THE DOGFATHER

This Large Print Book carries the
Seal of Approval of N.A.V.H.

A PAMPERED PETS MYSTERY

THE DOGFATHER

SPARKLE ABBEY

THORNDIKE PRESS

A part of Gale, a Cengage Company

Farmington Hills, Mich • San Francisco • New York • Waterville, Maine
Meriden, Conn • Mason, Ohio • Chicago

Copyright © 2018 by Carter Woods, LLC.
A Pampered Pets Mystery.
Thorndike Press, a part of Gale, a Cengage Company.

LIBRARY OF CONGRESS CIP DATA ON FILE.
CATALOGUING IN PUBLICATION FOR THIS BOOK
IS AVAILABLE FROM THE LIBRARY OF CONGRESS

ISBN-13: 978-1-4328-5958-9 (hardcover)

Published in 2018 by arrangement with BelleBooks, Inc.

Printed in Mexico
1 2 3 4 5 6 7 22 21 20 19 18

We dedicate *The Dogfather* to those who love and work with service dogs so others in need are able to live fulfilling, independent lives. Thank you.

CHAPTER ONE

"This is a bad idea."

"It's a fine idea," Grey Donovan, my on-again, off-again fiancé countered. We'd been "off" for months now. Eight to be exact. To be honest, our last break-up felt final. I didn't see us ever being "on" again. His unexpected arrival at my shop, Bow Wow Boutique, and subsequent offer to help me restock shelves at ten thirty in the morning, wouldn't convince me otherwise.

His assistance felt calculated, as if helping would persuade me to agree to his preposterous idea to use my shop as a surveillance base for his current undercover FBI assignment. White-collar crime, art theft to be specific, was his specialty. Everyone in Laguna Beach knew him as a local art gallery owner, which provided him with the perfect cover. Which begged the question, why couldn't he continue to use his gallery as his cover? I wouldn't ask; he wouldn't tell.

Just like he wouldn't say why my shop was the "perfect" location or what his assignment was about.

"Chocolate éclairs with a chai tea latte is a fine idea. A walk on the beach at sunrise is a fine idea. This" — I made a circle in the air between us — "this is crazy talk. And a conversation best not had in public." I looked toward the unlocked door, concerned a customer could enter at any moment.

His gaze followed mine. With a low voice he said, "If I remember correctly, you like crazy talk."

He wasn't going to give up. "Grey, it's awkward." My tone matched his.

"Workable." He pivoted on the heel of his Armani Oxfords, and with his back to me, effortlessly unpacked a cardboard box of gourmet dog treats. I guess he'd decided the conversation was over.

I made quick work of hanging the last handful of small collars then continued to watch Grey as he meticulously lined the cellophane-wrapped bundles of bone-shaped cookies on a top shelf.

"See how well we work together?" Grey handed me the empty box.

I tossed it aside and watched the box land next to an end-cap of pawlish, designer dog cologne, and hair dye. Apparently, the discussion wasn't finished. I sighed at his dogged tenacity.

"We got along because we weren't talking. I still think it's a bad idea. Everyone will want to know why you're spending time here. What am I supposed to tell them?"

He merely shrugged his broad shoulders. He wore a dark-blue Tom Ford power suit, looking solid and charismatic. "Don't tell them anything."

"Avoidance won't solve anything. You know this town. Everyone gossips, including my customers." As my Grandma Tillie used to say, "Gossip spreads faster than mildew in a wet basement."

"Tell them we're working things out."

"No one will buy it." The late-summer heat wave must have killed some of his brain cells. We certainly didn't sound like we were working out anything. We sounded like we were arguing.

"People believe what they want. We just have to make them want to believe the narrative."

I used to find his confidence sexy. Today it was annoying. "And how do we do that?" I could have kicked myself for taking the bait.

He offered a lazy smile. "Be ourselves —"

My skeptical laugh filled the room, cutting him off. "I'm pretty sure that's why we broke up in the first place." And the second place. And the third place.

"Okay." He shoved his hands in his pockets and thought for a moment as he watched the front door.

His brown hair, normally cut above the collar, was a few weeks past the usual scheduled monthly trim. Was he actually growing sideburns? Regardless of his more "relaxed look," he was as handsome as ever, but for the first time he looked out of place in my shop.

"We could use the break-ins. It wouldn't be out of character for me to spend more time here." His voice low, thoughtful.

The Laguna Bash 'n Dash was what the media had labeled the three break-ins. The first two had happened shortly after the stores had closed; the most recent one, in the early morning. Nothing had been taken — not money or merchandise. Just random break-ins. The last I'd heard, the police weren't closing in on a suspect, and the local business owners were on edge. Were the culprits bored juveniles looking for a cheap thrill? Or was someone looking for something specific and just hadn't found it yet? It was all very strange.

I had to admit, the situation had me uneasy, too. So uneasy, I'd been leaving my bulldog, Missy, at home instead of bringing her to the shop. Missy may look like a guard dog, but lacked the temperament. She'd rather be everyone's buddy. I'd never forgive myself if something happened to her.

"Here's an idea," I said, grasping at straws to end the conversation before we were interrupted. "Darby's studio is next door. Use her business as your base of operations. I'm sure you can come up with a believable lie as to why you need to be there frequently."

Darby Beckett, my best friend, owned Paw Prints Photography. Bless her heart, she was extremely loyal to me. I doubted she'd agree to let Grey spend a significant amount of time at her studio no matter what excuse he produced. But the suggestion was worth a try if it kept Grey out of my shop.

He rocked back on his heels. "You really don't want to do this, do you?"

I was taken aback at his genuine surprise. "No, I don't."

He whistled softly under his breath. "Melinda Langston, since when did you become risk adverse?"

I bristled at his accusation, even though I knew he was purposely egging me on. "You

11

won't goad me into agreeing."

I was a risk taker. I loved an adrenaline rush, the thrill of successfully tackling something just out of my reach. But what he proposed was dangerous to my heart, and that was different.

Grey leaned nonchalantly against the counter, his blue eyes alive with the competitive banter. His intense scrutiny made me itchy. I narrowed my eyes, scrutinizing him in return, trapping us into a game of who'd blink first.

"You're scared," he said.

Heck, yeah. But I'd never admit it to him.

"You know how I feel about lying. For us to pretend we're together when we're not, even for your secret operation . . ." I shrugged.

"It's important." The words "to me" hung in the air unspoken.

I blew the bangs from my eyes, determined to win this argument. "I understand. Let's be honest, you could hang around the boutique every day, for hours on end, while we pretend to be back together, but our friends, my customers . . . they won't buy it."

"I disagree. But I can compromise. How about this? I'm here to woo you back. It wouldn't be the first time."

Woo? Not the first time? What did that even mean? At least he didn't say "win" like I was a novelty carnival prize.

The front door of Bow Wow jerked opened, triggering the welcome bell. Thank the good Lord we were interrupted, because I had no idea how to respond to his off-the-cuff statement without saying something I would regret.

"What are you doing here, Handsome?" My eighty-something assistant, Betty Foxx, danced toward Grey, her raisin-lipstick-colored eyebrows lifted in joy. It was a new color, and in my humble opinion, one of her better choices. I'd never asked about the lipstick eyebrows. Whatever the reason for her unique makeup application, it would never live up to all the reasons I'd come up with on my own. Don't ask, don't be disap-pointed, was my sentiment.

When she reached his side, she raised a papery cheek for a quick kiss, which Grey willingly obliged. The smell of fresh coffee and lilacs surrounded her, and I wondered where she'd been.

"I'm here to see Mel —" he started.

"I thought you were going to be here an hour ago?" I directed my question to Betty before Grey could weave a charismatic story meant to serve his grand plan of making my shop his operations base.

Betty had been scheduled to open the boutique, but had texted early this morning that she had an errand to run and would be late. Knowing Betty, that errand could have been making a bank deposit or casing the bank for a future heist. You just never knew what the impish octogenarian was plotting. Even though she could be taxing at times, I adored her spunk to live her life to the fullest.

"After I took care of my *personal business,* I ran in to Mason Reed from the Hot Handbags store up the street. He wanted to know about the Mobster Film Festival sponsorship you were twisting his arm about."

The Mobster Film Festival was a fundraiser for Angels with Paws, a local nonprofit organization for seizure response dogs. Ella Johns, president and daughter of the founder, had asked if I would agree to secure sponsorships from Laguna businesses. As a fellow rescue supporter, how could I say no? I take my fundraising seriously.

"I wasn't twisting his arm," I said.

Betty threw me a "Get real" look.

"I was twisting *Quinn's* arm." Quinn, Mason's much younger wife, liked to spend money. I hoped she'd drop a few thousand in the Angels with Paws direction.

Betty snorted. "It's all the same to him. He's a little off, ya know what I mean?"

I did know, but entertaining that line of conversation would only drop us down a rabbit hole.

"So did you convince him?" Normally our tight-knit, downtown business owners were the first to give to a great cause, but due to the recent break-ins, most owners were reluctant to cough up money they might need later for repairs and replacing damaged merchandise.

"Of course I did. I told him you'd be over later today to pick up a check." She scooted past me and dropped her purse on the shelf under the counter. "Cookie didn't let you talk." She circled back to Grey, undeterred. "What are you two hiding?"

Grey flashed a good-humored smile. "Can't a guy stop by and check out the new merchandise?"

"You fostering a new dog I don't know about?" she asked.

"Not right now."

Betty propped her bony elbow on the counter, leaning closer to Grey. "Exactly. Spill it, Big Guy. Why are you here? We're not investigating any dead bodies, so you're not here to tell us to keep our noses clean. You and Cookie aren't doing the horizontal hokey pokey anymore since you broke her heart, so you're not here to make plans."

I choked back an automatic denial about my previous broken heart. "*Hello,* I'm standing right here."

Her raisin-colored eyebrows disappeared under her thinning white hair. "Am I wrong?"

Grey tipped his head toward me, the corners of his eyes crinkled with entertainment and subterfuge. I hated that I could decipher what he silently communicated. He was about to test the waters for his new cover story, and there was nothing I could do to stop him that wouldn't look suspicious.

"After the break-in at Baubles, I thought I'd check in and see how Mel was holding up."

"The jewelry store break-in happened three days ago." Betty dismissed his answer without a second thought. "Besides, Cookie's not your girlfriend anymore. She doesn't need you checking on her. Heck, you didn't do that a whole lot when you were together. We can take care of ourselves. You're up to something."

He held his palms upward. "I'm an open book."

She narrowed shrewd eyes, glaring in his direction. You could practically hear the wheels turning in her head. "I heard you were parading a new sweet thing around town last week. A tall blond. Not as good-looking as Cookie from what I hear. Maybe this mystery woman's got something to do with why you're here."

I couldn't stop my head from reflexively snapping to attention. What was Betty talking about?

Grey's eyes hardened, his voice terse. "Not true. If you hear that again, I'd appreciate it if you'd correct them."

"I gotcha," she cackled, pleased with herself. She slapped his arm. "You've finally admitted you were wrong and want Cookie back. That's why you're here. It's written all over your face. You can't hide anything from me. I got your number, Handsome."

The fist squeezing my heart relaxed, the ache quickly turning into annoyance. "Betty, you shouldn't joke about stuff like that." I eyed Grey and muttered under my breath, "This doesn't change anything."

They appraised me with knowing looks. Betty's unfounded conclusion only emboldened Grey's wild plan. I forced myself not

17

to flinch under their stares.

"You sound upset, Cookie. I thought you were over the big lug?" She didn't wait for a reply; instead she turned her attention to Grey. "I learned something else. Since you're back on Team Cookie, you should know Mason's claiming you sold him a junk picture."

Grey stiffened. "Is that so?"

"Now, don't get all worked up," Betty said. "I cleared that up for you even before I knew you were back on Team Cookie. I told him he didn't know what he was talking about; you don't sell flea market imitations. But you better follow up with that airbag. He's a mouthy handful."

Betty smoothed her wide-legged pajama bottoms, the blue floral print too big for her small frame. Yes, I said pajamas. There was a lot about Betty that didn't make sense, but for me that was part of her charm.

"Mason Reed thinks you've sold him forgeries?" I asked Grey. "Why would he think that?"

"It's under control."

I knew from experience his official FBI tone meant that was all he'd say. So I dropped it and took the unexpected opportunity to change the subject.

"Well . . . thanks for dropping by. I believe

18

you were just on your way out when Betty arrived."

"Cookie, are you wearing your cranky pants today?"

"Yes, and my butt has never looked better."

I expected Grey to leave, but his hesitation suggested he wanted to say something. He glanced at Betty once more then said to me, "We'll talk later."

"I bet you'll do more than talking." Betty laughed at her innuendo.

Grey winked at her. "If I'm lucky."

"Enough, enough." I ushered him out the door. I wondered if he would slip next door to talk to Darby like I'd suggested. He gave me one last look, an expression I didn't want to decipher, and then walked in the opposite direction.

"You were hard on him, Cookie. Still haven't forgiven him, eh?"

"You didn't mention where you went this morning."

Betty hmphed. "You're not my keeper. What are you gonna do about those boxes you left in front of the pawlish? I can't sell product if you're trashing up the place."

I smiled. We were both deflecting. I grabbed the empty cardboard boxes I had tossed aside earlier and stacked them in the storeroom. I'd break them down and toss them in the recycling dumpster behind the building later. I had an errand to run first.

"Betty, hold down the fort for a bit. I'm going to walk over to Hot Handbags to pick up that check for the festival before Mason changes his mind."

"Good idea. You gotta catch him while you can. He's a slippery one." She kept her back to me as she answered, obviously not wanting me to see her shove a small sheet of paper inside her purse. Interesting. Mason wasn't the only slippery character in my orbit today.

The summer sun had burned through the typical ocean-side morning fog by the time I started the short two-block walk up the street to Hot Handbags. I inhaled deeply, breathing in the salty air. Bumper-to-bumper traffic, crowded sidewalks, and bad parking jobs — all a dead giveaway that it was tourist season. I wasn't complaining. For this Texas-born SoCal transplant and self-proclaimed beachaholic, it was another beautiful day in paradise.

Except for dealing with Mason. He looked like a trustworthy guy with his "Who me?" shrugs and seemingly interested head tilt as you were conversing. Once you got past the

façade, you realized he was arrogant, super-
ficial at best, and enjoyed a sly put-down at
someone else's expense. Nor did he give his
time or money for the betterment of the
community without something in return.
Maybe I was overly suspicious. If you asked
my mama, she'd be the first to agree.

In their defense, Mason and Quinn Reed
were relatively new to Laguna, having arrived about a year earlier. That could explain
their reluctance to jump head first into
overly active community committees,
church socials, and local fundraisers. But it
had been a year. Certainly they'd had plenty
of time to get their bearings. There was
something fishy about those two, mostly
Mason, only I couldn't put my finger on
what it was. Yet.

With the Laguna Mobster Film Festival a
month away, I'd been after the Reeds to
donate something — a handbag, a wallet, a
keychain — anything we could auction off.
Each time I'd approached Quinn, she'd
always responded the same. "I'm sure we'll
do something." But the way she'd said it
felt more like a brush-off than a commitment of any kind.

Once I had realized I wasn't making
progress with the direct approach, I altered
my strategy and targeted Mason's ego. As a

sponsor, he could simply write a check, and his name and business logo would be plastered all over town. No extra participation required. Unfortunately, that hadn't worked either.

Yet somehow Betty had convinced Mason to cough up five grand. I was still trying to wrap my mind around it. A part of me wondered if Mason had really agreed to a sponsorship or if Betty had heard what she wanted to hear and I was about to be thrown out on my behind.

I pushed open the heavy glass door of Hot Handbags. A rush of cold air-conditioned air swept over me as I walked inside. My heart skipped a beat at the site before me. I had a thing for purses. Looking around the smallish boutique, my fingers twitched wanting to touch the gorgeous bags lined up along the back-lit shelving units attached to the walls. Chanel. Louis Vuitton. Tory Burch. Kate Spade. Stella McCartney. Gucci. Hermès. Coach. The smell of luxury — expensive leather and designer perfume — clung to the air.

A handful of customers milled around the store, gently caressing the high-end accessories. Well, maybe not caressing, but definitely treating the merchandise with reverence.

I spotted Quinn descending the contemporary wrought-iron staircase in the back of the store. She looked every inch the television version of an Orange County housewife in her white cigarette pants and black, sleeveless, eyelet top. Her five-inch heel caught the edge of the bottom stair; she stumbled, grabbing the railing to right herself. One of the women fawning over a Stella McCartney velvet shoulder bag gasped.

I rushed over to Quinn. "Are you okay?"

She brushed away my hands. "I'm fine, thank you." She smoothed the beach-blond locks flowing over her shoulders. She gave me the once-over, wordlessly pronouncing judgment with a raised brow. My "I don't need therapy, I have a dog" t-shirt, jeans, and flats were found underwhelming.

She gingerly placed weight on her foot. Seeming uninjured, she strutted into the middle of the store. "Is there something you needed, Mel?" she asked over her shoulder.

I smothered the annoyance bubbling inside me. I swallowed my pride and followed like an obedient puppy.

"Betty told me that you and Mason have agreed to sponsor the Angels with Paws event next month, and I needed to pick up the check this morning. We really appreciate your contribution. The film festival is gearing up to be a huge success."

Quinn rolled her striking green eyes. "Your grandmother can be rather dogged when she wants something."

A burst of laughter escaped me. "She would say older sister, but we're not related. She works at the boutique. Betty has become invested in the festival the last couple of months. She's hoping for a good turnout so Sal Poochino will make an appearance."

Quinn's plastic smile told me she'd stopped listening.

I released a deep breath and started over. "Anyway, if I could just grab that check, I'll get out of your hair and you can get back to your customers."

"Wait here." She spun around and headed back to the staircase she'd almost tumbled down minutes earlier.

I weaved through a number of displays, making my way closer to a couple of other customers who were whispering like star-crossed teenagers.

"It's wearable art," the short brunette whispered reverently.

"Oh, you'd be Queen Bee of Omaha with the Gucci shoulder bag. You have to buy it!" The tall black-haired gal picked up the bag and shoved it at her friend.

Summer tourists made the best customers. Their enthusiasm was contagious. A Christian Louboutin, silver leather clutch caught my eye. It was every handbag snob's dream. Love at first sight. Casual sophistication. Modern. The perfect complement to a pair of metallic Rene Caovilla sandals in my closet.

As I internally debated the purchase of the handbag, the front door opened and Nina Fernandez, a loyal customer of Bow Wow Boutique and lover of all canines, strolled inside. The second she saw me, her brown eyes widened, and a bright smile spread across her red lips. She rushed toward me, unknowingly saving me from dropping an obscene amount of money.

When she reached my side, we shared a couple of customary Nina cheek kisses. Right then left. Her slicked-back, long ponytail swung from side to side.

"Mel, I was just at your shop." She held up a small Bow Wow bag. "Betty just sold me on the cutest plush monkey toy. Dash will love it."

"You got away without buying a bottle of doggie cologne? I'm shocked." Dash was the most adorable dachshund puppy. His soulful eyes melted my heart every time he stopped by the shop.

Nina waved her free hand nonchalantly through the air. "Oh, that's just a given. You know Dash likes to smell good for the ladies. It's so great to see you. How's Missy? I noticed she hasn't been at the shop the last couple times I've been there."

"She's good. I haven't felt comfortable bringing her in since the last break-in."

Nina's eyes widened. "Any news on who's behind that?"

I shook my head. "Not that I've heard."

"Even with your direct line?"

I laughed, a tad uncomfortable. She was referring to my unusual relationship with Homicide Detective Judd Malone. "That line only picks up when dead bodies are involved."

She patted my arm reassuringly. "I guess it's good that there are no dead bodies then." She sighed dramatically. "I am worried that if the police don't catch whoever is behind these nuisance crimes we'll lose the foot traffic downtown. We can't afford that."

"I know. I'm sure the police are doing everything they possibly can. We just need to be patient."

Easier said than done. I couldn't say that I was afraid to be alone at the shop, but I did worry about Betty at times. She believed she was invincible; capable of defending

26

herself (she's taken self-defense classes) and anyone else who happened to be inside the store should we become the target. I'd experienced the gun-toting, bad-kung-fu-moves side of Betty. A little erratic and unpredictable was the kindest description I could come up with. Not a good look for anyone.

Nina looked around quizzically. "Are Mason or Quinn around?"

"I haven't seen Mason, but Quinn's upstairs grabbing a check for the film festival next month."

Nina looked surprised. "They gave you money?"

I shrugged. "Betty managed to get Mason to agree."

She leaned in close. "Did she blackmail him?" she whispered.

If she'd asked that about anyone else, I'd have laughed and brushed it off. But Betty was involved. History had taught me, anything was possible if she believed the end result important enough.

"I'm sure she just wore him down. You know what she's like when she makes up her mind." I quickly changed the subject. "We can count on you and Dash to attend the festival next month, right?"

"Of course we'll be there. I already know

27

what he should wear to the special viewing of *The Godfather*. I love that we're dressing our dogs as our favorite character. Such a grand idea."

I smiled. "I'd love to take credit for it, but I can't."

"I need to bring Dash to the boutique to try on the costume I have in mind. Maybe tomorrow? And you can show me what Missy's going to wear."

"Absolutely. I can't wait to see which one you've picked. I haven't decided on something for Missy. Of course Betty has something over the top in mind for Raider." Raider was Betty's full-of-life Saint Bernard. He was two years old and almost as big as Betty. She'd been working with my lovely cousin, Caro Lamont, pet behaviorist extraordinaire, to learn how to control Raider. It was a work in progress. So was my relationship with my cousin.

We continued to chat about upcoming events. I could hear a landline ringing upstairs. Suddenly, Quinn's cold voice thundered from upstairs. Nina trailed off, and we looked at each other, awkwardly eavesdropping. I shrugged, not sure what would have triggered Quinn to lose her cool knowing she had customers in the store. I couldn't make out what she was saying, but her tone was aggressive. Whoever was on the other end was getting an earful.

Nina cleared her throat and made her excuses, then meandered toward the front of the shop. I should have followed her, but my inquiring mind wasn't so easily distracted. It didn't matter. As soon as the yelling had started, it stopped. I felt a twinge of disappointment the show was over.

Oh wow! I sounded like Betty. There was a sobering thought.

Speaking of Betty, I wished I'd brought my cell phone along. There was no telling what she had been up to in my absence.

Within a few minutes I could hear the familiar clip-clop sound trailing down the staircase. I walked in her direction, praying she wouldn't stumble on the last step again. Quinn was mumbling something under her breath as she made her way downstairs.

I met her at the bottom step. She released a deep breath, regaining her composure. Whatever that phone call had been about, it had definitely shaken her.

She was also empty handed.

Before I could say anything, she shook her head. "It seems Mason has the checkbook. Unfortunately, I cannot write that check after all."

She looked flustered. Because of the

phone argument or because of the missing checkbook? Hard to know.

"I can come back later this afternoon," I pressed.

Her cheek twitched. "Tomorrow. I have a spa day scheduled in the morning. Mason can take care of his own mess."

Here it was. Betty had heard what she wanted to hear. "He's changed his mind?" I hedged.

She brushed her long bangs to the side of her face, tucking them behind her ear. "I told you we'd do something. Apparently, Mason decided on a sponsorship. He'll have a check for you."

"Signed?" I don't know what made me think to say that, but it didn't seem out of character for them to invent excuses to not part with the money.

She stiffened. "Of course."

"Wonderful. Nothing could keep me away."

CHAPTER TWO

Well, I hadn't been thrown out on my bum, but I was heading back to the shop without a check. I'd like to say I was surprised, but that would be a lie. Anyone who knew me knew I hated lying. Partly because I was a horrible liar. Mostly because lying led to secrets, and in my experience, secrets led to dead bodies.

The outdoor crowds had grown larger in the short time I was with Quinn. If the number of people walking their dogs was an indicator of our possible business, we'd see a crush of customers this afternoon.

The challenge of living in a popular tourist town was that the crowds never moved swiftly down the street. Walking was more like being trapped in a group of bored party guests holding up the back wall while they observed the action on the dance floor.

A half block down the road I saw Darby and her Afghan hound, Fluffy, slip inside my boutique. Excited to see my best friend, I hotfooted it the rest of the way. I slipped around a group of bubbly teenage girls huddled together for a selfie in front of the surf shop. I may have "accidently" photo-bombed them, not that they noticed.

I entered the boutique with a smile on my face. That smile was short lived.

Betty, Darby, Grey, and none other than Mason Reed were poised to rumble. That might be a slight exaggeration. I quickly assessed the group, and judging by the body language, they weren't about to perform a *Dancing with the Stars* group routine. What looked to have been a heated conversation had stalled at my entrance.

Mason's uncharacteristic disheveled appearance — wrinkled khakis, misbuttoned Tommy Bahama shirt — matched his unruly attitude. It was possible he'd already been in one fight and was spoiling for another. His hands were braced on the counter, as if ready to leap across at the slightest provocation. Is it bad that I wondered if he had the check for Angels with Paws with him? Too soon for that line of questioning?

"Did you start the party without me?" I strove to bring some humor to the tense situation.

"This ain't no party, Cookie. Mason here

is causing trouble." Betty sent a scowl in Mason's direction. She had positioned herself behind the counter next to Grey, imitating his imposing stance, but not pulling it off.

Darby, in a white cotton shirt, tweed shorts, and Diane Keaton-inspired polka-dot scarf, had her back to me, almost hiding behind a round table of fabric dog mannequins and jeweled collars. She looked over her shoulder and silently communicated with a small tilt of her head toward Grey. He was in protector mode. His square jaw tightened as I made my way toward them.

Well, crapola. I was in a rather precarious position. I wanted money from Mason, but I certainly didn't want him scaring away my customers with his drama.

"Mason was just leaving, Melinda." Grey didn't take his eyes off Mason.

"I'm not leaving until you admit that painting is a forgery."

Darby slid out from behind the table. "Is there a reason you can't have this discussion at the gallery? I'm sure neither of you intend to scare away Mel's customers."

God bless my best friend. The girl always had my back. I mouthed "thank you" to her. Fluffy stood next to Darby, perfectly erect, pointy nose stuck in the air, signifying she was ready to leave even if the guys weren't. Snob Dog's personality was the complete opposite of Darby.

Mason remained rooted in place. "I've attempted to have this conversation at your gallery, but you weren't there. You haven't been there for days," he bit out.

"The building has wiring issues. You have my number. You could have called me."

Well, that was news to me. The wiring part, not the phone number.

I stood next to Mason, diverting his attention away from Grey and toward me. "I just came from your store. Betty had mentioned you'd agreed to become a sponsor for the festival next month. I'm glad she was able to change your mind."

He dropped his hands and finally looked in my direction. "Did I?" He tilted his head and offered me a lopsided smile.

Although his demeanor looked accommodating, I didn't trust him for a second.

Betty leaned across the counter. "Don't try to weasel out of it. You agreed. Now hold up your end of the agreement." She wagged a bony finger in his direction.

"I'll give you that check . . . when *he* admits what he did."

"I didn't do anything." Grey's tone

34

brooked no argument.

"All right, that's it." I couldn't afford for the drama to continue. I had a business to run. "Everyone out of my shop except for Darby and Betty."

Fluffy swung her head around, leveling a haughty gaze at me.

I sighed. "Fine. You can stay, too."

Betty patted Grey's arm. "Sorry, Handsome, but you know how Cookie can get. You better listen to her. You just got back into her good graces. You gotta do what she wants if you're gonna stick around."

"Really? You're going to continue to talk about me like I'm not here? For how long?" I asked Betty.

"I'm on Handsome's side for this one." She winked at Grey.

"I want my money back." Mason didn't budge, uninterested in Betty's and my bickering.

"I'll give it back when you return the painting I sold you and not that knock-off you're parading around town." Grey's words were measured. His sharp blue eyes drilling into Mason.

A collective gasp filled the air as we realized what Grey was implying. Was this why he wanted to use my shop for his secret undercover assignment? Was Mason involved in some type of art forgery and Grey was trying to keep an eye on his store?

The front door opened, and the bell chimed, cutting through the tension. A couple of teens I had walked past earlier waltzed inside, speed-talking about all the things they had seen this morning. I glared at the two men, warning them to shut up and take their argument somewhere else.

"Welcome to Bow Wow Boutique," Betty greeted the girls warmly. She slipped past Grey and skillfully made her way toward the customers. "Is there anything in particular you ladies are looking for? I see you both have lovely nails. By any chance would you be interested in some pawlish for your pampered pooch?"

While Betty distracted the girls, I turned my attention to Grey and Mason. "I'm not kidding. If you two are going to argue, leave. Mason, Quinn said you had the checkbook. I would appreciate it if you could write a check to the Angels with Paws before you leave."

"I don't know what you're talking about. I don't have the checkbook. The only time it leaves the store is if the bookkeeper has it." Mason's clipped tone expressed his irritation.

Well, Hell's Bells. I didn't know what to

think. One of them was trying to play me for a fool.

"Like I mentioned earlier, you gentlemen are welcome to continue this discussion next door," Darby said.

Fluffy let out a huge sigh and leaned her long body against Darby's legs. The Afghan hound could not have looked any more bored. Darby patted her head gently and murmured something to her.

Grey abruptly checked his watch. "I have an appointment across town. Mason, once you return the original, I will give you a full refund. Don't try to fool me again. You won't get away with it."

Mason's face burned crimson. I could almost feel the heat of his anger radiating from him.

"We'll see who gets away," he muttered.

Grey moved from behind the counter and walked toward the door. As he passed Mason, Mason reached into the pocket of his wrinkled pants.

My heart raced. "Grey," I yelled.

Grey whipped around ready to defend himself. Mason jumped, startled. His cell phone dropped from his hand, slapping the hardwood floor.

Well, that couldn't have been any more awkward. I guess all the break-ins had me more on edge than I realized.

"What did you think I was going to pull out of my pocket?" Mason angrily snatched up his phone and inspected it.

I couldn't get my breath to push past the lump in my throat.

"Obviously, she thought you had a gun, you yahoo," Betty said from across the room.

The two teens Betty had loaded up with a basket of merchandise stood frozen, eyes wide, their gazes zipping back and forth between me and Betty. They looked horrified. I felt the same. I wasn't even sure how to save this one.

I cleared my throat and found my voice.

"Free dog treats, everyone?"

It was early evening when I pulled in to my driveway, turned off the Jeep's engine, then rested my head against the hard steering wheel. I had survived the day from hell. It wasn't the worst day I'd ever experienced. I mean, there were no dead bodies, so technically it could have been worse. But it was still a bad day.

I had three things on my mind to end the day on a positive note: cuddling with Missy, a large glass of red wine, and a hot bath — not necessarily in that order.

I grabbed my Chloé tote, got out of the car, and made my way to the house. There was still plenty of sunlight so I could take Missy for a quick walk before I shut down for the night and soaked in the tub. I opened my front door and practically fell into the house, tripping over Missy. Before I could close the door, she barreled past me, tongue hanging out of her mouth, and into the front yard.

"Whoa! Get back in here," I shouted.

Missy charged down the sidewalk, past the next-door neighbor, like a prisoner escapee.

I tossed my purse onto the couch and then raced after my crazy dog.

The nice thing about bulldogs: they don't run very fast, and they burn through their energy quickly. Worn out, Missy dropped under a eucalyptus tree just two houses up the street.

"What's wrong with you?" I asked when I reached her.

Pant, pant, pant.

"Why are you being so naughty?"

Pant, pant, pant. Snort.

She hadn't acted this poorly since she was a pup. I squatted next to her and stroked her back. She rolled over, offering her soft belly for a rub or perhaps an apology. My

39

heart rate slowed down as I petted her. We both sighed.

"Are you ready to go home?" I asked softly.

She got to her feet and shook.

I smiled. "All right, let's go."

Feeling guilty for being gone so long and not taking her to the shop with me, I picked her up and carried her home. Forty pounds of solid bulldog — I considered it my upper body workout for the day.

Once we were inside the house, with the door closed, I set her down. She immediately bumbled over to her dog bowls in the kitchen. While she chomped her kibble, I refilled her water dish.

I kicked off my flats, shoving them under a bar stool. The hardwood floor felt cool under my bare feet. One of the best things about living alone was you could leave your belongings wherever you wanted.

I grabbed a bottle of red wine off the rack on the counter and pulled a wine glass out of the cupboard. I uncorked the bottle and filled the glass. I took a long drink, savoring the warmth that traveled down my throat. Check off the first item from my to-do list for the night.

Missy was still chowing down, so I decided to draw a bath. We could cuddle on the couch later. I topped off my glass and then made my way to the master bathroom. I took one step into my room and almost choked on my wine.

It looked like a tornado had blown through. Missy had eaten her way through a box of facial tissues until only wet remnants of blue papers were strewn across the carpet. The stack of "to-be-read books" on my nightstand had been knocked off onto the floor. My treasured collection of designer shoes had been terrorized. I picked up my favorite pair of Stuart Weitzman motorcycle boots. I felt sick. One boot had become a leather chew toy and was beyond repair. What had been a positive, leaving my belongings anywhere I wanted, had suddenly become an opportunity for naughty bulldog behavior.

Missy toddled behind me and burped loudly. I stared her down. She licked her lips, not looking the least bit ashamed of the war zone she'd created in my bedroom.

I choked back my frustration. "Why can't you sleep at home like you do at the shop?"

My boots were beyond saving. I closed my eyes as I tossed them into the trash. It hurt to admit, but her bad behavior was due to my decision to keep her home. She didn't understand the change in her routine, and I hadn't prepared her well. She missed me, missed the shop, and she was bored.

Missy had found her way to the bed. After a prolonged downward dog stretch, she lay down with her head between her paws, content to watch me clean up her crime scene. I was in the midst of gathering the scattered mystery books and stacking them on top of my nightstand when I heard the faint ringing of my cell phone. My tote was still on the couch where I'd left it, phone inside. I ignored the call and continued to collect half-eaten tissues.

It wasn't but a minute later when the phone rang again. Whoever it was calling was persistent. I headed for the living room. I heard Missy jump down from the bed and follow me. I pulled my cell from my purse and checked the caller ID. Mama. We hadn't talked for almost a month. A blissfully drama-free month. I loved my mama, and I knew in her way she loved me, too, but our relationship was . . . complicated.

I answered my phone. "Hey, Mama."

"Is that your lovely voice, Melinda Sue? I wasn't sure for a minute. It's been so long since we've talked. Bless your heart for calling to let me know you're still alive." Mama could be charming while simultaneously disagreeable.

Where was my wine? "If I was dead, Betty would have called you."

She sucked in a breath. "That's not funny, Melinda." If my Mama was Catholic, I imagined this was when she'd cross herself and glance heavenward praying for my damned soul.

I curled up on the couch, patting the cushion next to me, inviting Missy to join me. "How are you? How's Daddy?"

"Your daddy is working too hard. He's been saying he's fixin' to retire for two years now, but he keeps scooting off to the office every morning."

I tried to imagine Jack Langston retired. I drew a blank. "What would he do?"

There was a dramatic pause on the other end of the phone. Now I'd stepped in it. The real reason for her call. I braced myself for whatever was about to happen.

"He could take me to visit my only grandbaby." She managed to sound defiant yet offended at the same time.

Since I wasn't pregnant nor adopting, she had to be talking about my brother Mitch and his wife Nikki. A much-needed smile blossomed across my lips. I was going to be an auntie. "Mitch and Nikki are having a baby? When?"

I could hear her moving items around.

Slamming drawers. Possibly packing?

"Last month."

"Oh," I said softly. Missy rested her head on my feet.

Mama was fired up, and for once it was possible she wasn't overreacting. I had a feeling I knew the answer, which would explain this call, but I asked anyway.

"Mama, forgive me for asking a sensitive question, but how long have you known about the baby?"

"Eight minutes," she declared, her Texas drawl more pronounced than I'd heard in a while. "I withered in pain for twenty-eight hours in labor with Mitch. The least he could do is invite me to the birth of my first grandbaby. But he kept me away. Am I so awful that he needed to keep me in the dark about something so important? At least they had the decency to return to the states and not have my grandbaby in London. My goodness, I had no idea Nikki was even pregnant. Why does your brother hate me?" She hiccupped, choking back tears.

It didn't matter what the situation was about; when it came down to it, in the end, it was always about Mama, which was probably why Mitch had waited to share his good news. The minute Mama had learned of Nikki's pregnancy, Mama would have flown to England and been standing at their front door, ready to take over.

"No one hates you," I reassured her.

She collected herself. "Tell me the truth. I can take it. Did you know about the baby?"

"No. They didn't mention the baby in any of their emails. You know Mitch is like me. We like . . . privacy." It was the nicest way I could say that we had moved thousands of miles away from her because she was nosey. Bossy. Controlling. Although I was a tad hurt they'd kept me in the dark too, I tended to believe it was so I'd have plausible deniability once they did tell our mother.

"I am your mama. You don't get to have privacy from me."

And that attitude explained it all. "So when are you leaving?"

"I'm not going anywhere. They're coming home for a visit. I've already called Hector to design a nursery. I was thinking all white, with gold accents. Lace of course. Maybe velvet."

There was no stopping her. If daddy was a workaholic now, he'd pick up two new projects to stay out of the line of fire during the nursery remodel.

"When are they coming?"

"The end of the month. You need to come home too. This is important. Don't break your daddy's heart."

My mother had been working me to come home for a visit for the past two years. Each time she'd bring up disappointing my daddy. I'd managed to come up with an excellent excuse each time. So good, in fact, that one day Mama just appeared on my doorstep. Technically, it was Grey's doorstep, but it still wasn't in Texas. This was probably the only way she'd get me to come home.

I loved my brother. I loved my sister-in-law. And I loved my . . .

"Do I have a niece or nephew?"

Mama's voice softened. "Girl. Elmsly Tillie Langston."

My brother had named his daughter after our Grandma Tillie. My heart swelled with love for my niece. I had so much to teach her. "Yes."

I was greeted with silence. "Did you just agree?"

I laughed so loudly, Missy picked her head up and stared at me. "Yes, I did. I'll come home to the great state of Texas to meet my niece."

"Melinda Sue, you better not be teasing me. My heart couldn't take it." I could hear tears catch in her throat. "Are you really coming home?"

"A visit. It's just a visit," I clarified. "Don't get any ideas, Mama."

"I'll have Daddy send the jet for you —"

Good grief. She just didn't slow down. "No, no, no. I'll drive out and bring Missy. I won't stay long. I do have a business to run." I needed to talk to Betty to work out some type of schedule for the shop. Darby might be willing to help out, too.

"That's why you hired that Betty woman. Bring Grey along. He can help you drive."

"Mama!"

"Okay, okay. I thought he would have come to his senses by now."

We ended the call on a positive note. It was a nice change. Hmm . . . maybe I needed to rethink my resistance regarding Grey using my shop as his operations base. I could do him a favor and in return, ride herd on Betty while I was gone.

The end of the month was less than two weeks away. Certainly I could take being in close quarters with Grey for ten days? Grey was a stand-up guy. Any ground rules I laid out, he would follow.

What could possibly go wrong?

I awoke the next morning with a plan to talk to Darby about my unexpected trip to Dallas, and the probability of Grey spending a significant amount of time at the shop. Betty's unpredictability was the key to bringing it all together. While that worked as a cover for Grey, it made me nervous for what mischief Betty might whip up, unbeknownst to Grey in my absence. I needed to cover my bases by asking Darby if she could help, too. Not long ago, I was gone for only two days, and Betty managed to order four thousand dollars' worth of dog sweaters. Her heart was in the right place trying to help me replenish our inventtory, except it was July. We still had unsold merchandise.

Betty had been scheduled to open today, but once again she had a personal errand and needed me to cover. She'd also sent me a text reminding me to pick up a couple of bottles of hand sanitizer from the drug store. She was purposely confused as to who was in charge.

I stopped by the Koffee Klatch to grab drinks for Darby and myself before making my way to Darby's studio. Paw Prints was just as unique as she was. I loved the unfinished warehouse, perfect for a variety of photo shoots, storing an abundance of props and equipment, and a lobby, which she had designed and staged like a Victorian-era parlor.

When I arrived, Darby was editing photos. I joined her in the makeshift office, a square card table and metal folding chair temporarily planted in the lobby. Since she did the majority of her editing at home, she insisted setting up the card table sufficed for those times she edited at the studio. I kept trying to convince her to build an actual office, but she hadn't been convinced.

Darby accepted the caramel latte I offered her. She plucked off the lid and sniffed the hot liquid. "It smells delicious. You're a life saver." She tossed the lid in the trash before taking a sip.

I dropped my tote bag on the velvet couch and settled in. Or at least tried to. The thin cushion wasn't much padding against the mahogany frame. "You know, this isn't very comfortable." I searched the studio. "Speaking of uncomfortable, where's Fluffy?"

"She's with the trainer auditioning for a Disney movie. If she gets the role, filming starts next month."

"Really?"

Darby tossed me a flippant look over her shoulder. "Don't sound so excited. It's only for a few days."

Fluffy was an award-winning dog actor. I always said "dog actor" with a British accent, because it sounded pretentious — just

49

like Fluffy. Darby inherited the snooty Afghan hound shortly after moving here from Omaha. I will admit, since the two had been together, Fluffy had dialed back her snobbery.

"Hey, if she gets the part, any chance she can introduce Betty to a few human stars?"

Darby laughed lightly. "I'll see what I can do." She turned her attention back to her computer. "So, I was surprised to see Grey at your shop yesterday."

"You weren't the only one," I muttered. I kicked off my flats then tucked my feet underneath me. I shifted, attempting to get comfortable. "You really need a different couch."

She raised her brow. "I didn't realize you were seeing each other again."

"Me and the couch?" I could tell by her blank expression, she wasn't impressed with my humorous deflection. "We're not."

Darby turned in her chair and faced me. "I see. Did you leave Missy home again?"

I wasn't fooled. Her change in topic was only temporary. She wasn't about to let me off that easy. Not when it came to Grey.

"Yeah. But she's struggling. And I'm feeling really guilty."

"Separation anxiety?"

I nodded. "For both of us." I sighed. "She

50

chewed my motorcycle boots yesterday."

Darby's eyes widened. "Oh, no."

"My favorite pair. I feel like I should have held a funeral before I tossed them."

"Poor thing. Missy must have been really stressed out."

"It's my fault. I've got to figure something out." I took a sip of my chai latte.

"If you were my client, I'd recommend that you contact Caro." She paused when I choked on my drink. "But since you and your cousin aren't speaking, you could ask Colin to take on Missy."

I ignored her Caro reference. "Colin?"

Darby blushed. "Remember that blind date I went on a few weeks ago? Well, we're still seeing each other."

I smiled. "So it's going well enough you'll let me meet him? Are we instituting the best friend stamp of approval plan?"

She shook her head with a laugh. "While a second opinion is typically good, I just thought he could help you out."

"Is he a dog behaviorist?"

"A dog sitter. He has a website, Dog Days. He's actually really good with Fluffy."

"Really? Does she know that?"

"Eh . . ." She twisted her lips. "She doesn't hate him."

"Well . . ." I laughed. "He must be a winner then."

Her face lit up as she spoke. "He has the best Golden Retriever, Bryan Goosling. He's adorable and acts like he has no idea he's a dog."

"Bryan Goosling?" Judging by what Colin had named his dog, he could possibly be the perfect fit for Darby. "He likes chick flicks?"

"He likes all types of movies. I'll ask him to stop by the shop this afternoon. Talk to him. See what you think."

"Hey, I'll try almost anything at this point. Not to change the subject, but my mother called last night, for an actual reason."

A horrified look crossed her face. "She's coming to Laguna again?"

My eyes widened in equal horror. "Thank the good Lord, no."

I sat up and set my feet on the cold concrete floor. A happy grin pulled at my lips. "I'm an auntie. I have a niece."

She jumped up and hugged me. "How exciting! Congratulations. Is the new little family coming for a visit?"

I shook my head. "I'm going to Dallas at the end of the month." I patted the couch for Darby to sit next to me. "Look, I was hoping you could do me a favor and keep an eye on Betty and the shop."

"Of course. I'll check my schedule. How long will you be gone for?"

"No more than a week if that works for you and Betty."

"I'm sure we can work something out."

"You're the best. I know Betty can be a handful. I was thinking about asking Grey to pop in too. You know she adores him and will do whatever he wants. What do you think?"

Darby's excited expression transformed into concern. "Is that the only reason you'd ask him to come by?"

"What other reason would there be?"

"I don't know. What about him and Mason yesterday? Do you know what that was about?"

I shook my head. "That's the first I'd heard of anything underhanded with Mason. I have to tell you, I've always had my suspicions about him. He triggers my spidey senses. Grey and I may not be together anymore, but you and I know he's an honorable guy, and would never try to pass off a copy as an original painting."

"But you obviously still care deeply for Grey. You freaked out when you thought Mason was going to hurt him with his cell phone."

I caught the laughter in her words. I

53

cringed. "I might have overreacted."

"You think so?"

"You know the break-ins have me on edge. And honestly, I would have reacted the same way if I thought you or Betty were in danger." I could hear my own deflecting and backpedaling loud and clear.

My cell rang, saving me from continuing to dig myself a deeper hole of denial. I grabbed the phone from my tote and checked caller ID.

"It's Betty. Probably calling with a new excuse for why she's late. She's up to something."

Darby laughed. "When isn't she?"

"Good point," I mumbled. "I thought you were coming directly to the shop? What are you doing?" I spoke into the phone.

"Cookie." Betty's animated voice blasted in my ear. "You're never going to guess what I found."

"Hand sanitizer?" I deadpanned.

I could hear her heavy breathing on the other end. It wasn't her normal excited breathing. This was I-might-be-in-trouble type breathing. I caught Darby's eye.

She mouthed, "What?"

I shrugged and mouthed back, "I don't know."

"Betty, what's going on?"

54

Her voice raised a handful of octaves. "I wanted that check Mason promised. When I got to Hot Handbags, the door was unlocked even though they weren't open for another hour. I figured they were having an early-bird sale so I moseyed inside. I could pick up the check and maybe a new handbag."

"Of course."

"Well, there was no sale. I called for Mason, but he didn't answer."

My stomach tightened. "And?" I prompted her to finish.

"That's when I saw Amazon Barbie bent over Mason's dead body at the bottom of the stairs. He looked like a broken mannequin."

CHAPTER THREE

I rubbed my hand over my face. Betty excitedly described the mysterious Amazon Barbie who she was certain was a shoplifter or part of the Bash 'n Dash break-ins. I shoved my feet in my flats, jumped off the couch, and grabbed my purse. Darby looked at me a bit confused.

"Betty, take a breath." I turned to Darby and said, "Mason's dead. I'll fill you in later." I rushed out the door.

"I hope you called the police before you called me," I said back to the phone.

"Of course I did!" Betty defended. "Officer Hostas is already here. I overheard him say the victim fell down the stairs —"

"Do not touch Mason. I'm on my way."

Betty sighed. "I know my way around a body. It's not me you should worry about. It's that Amazon blond hunched over him. She wouldn't stop touching him. Slapped his cheek, shook his shoulders. Hey, the cops can't be mad at me for messing with their crime scene. It was all her."

I rushed up the street toward the Hot Handbags boutique for the second time in as many days. "Crime scene? I thought you just said he'd fallen down the stairs."

"Exactly. Otherwise, I would have called Detective Hottie."

"If it's an accident, it's not a crime scene." I could hear a commotion of some type in the background. "Look, I'm almost there. Why don't you meet me outside?"

"I think I'll just stay right where I am and keep an eye on Amazon Barbie. She's sketchy." Betty ended the call before I could protest.

I know she said it was an accident, and I had witnessed Quinn stumble on the last couple of steps just the day before, but I couldn't help wondering if Mason's death had anything to do with the break-ins. Did he stumble across an intruder? I didn't know him well enough to know if he had any enemies, or who Amazon Barbie was that Betty kept referring to, but she wasn't his wife.

By the time I made it to Hot Handbags, Officer Hostas's partner was outside keeping people out of the store. I slowed my pace, catching my breath and working out an explanation for my presence.

Apparently, I didn't need an excuse. As soon as he saw me he said, "Your girl Betty is inside, and she refuses to come out. Grab her and take her back to your store."

Yes, he recognized me.

I told him I'd be happy to take my assistant off his hands and quickly slipped inside before he changed his mind about letting me enter.

Betty was a short gal, barely five feet, with white curly hair. Easy to pick out when she was around people her size. At times like this, when everyone towered over her, it was hard to see where she could possibly be.

I spotted several uniformed police who milled around the store. I immediately recognized the woman Betty referred to as Amazon Barbie. She stuck out like a nylon duffle bag hanging with a handful of expensive leather shoulder purses. Amazon Barbie was the perfect description for the six-foot-something blond, with a thick braided rope of hair hanging down her back.

I could hear Officer Hostas's raised voice toward the back of the store. He was ordering someone — I assumed it was Betty — to stand back from Mason. As I got closer I realized it wasn't Betty at all Officer Hostas was talking to, but Amazon Barbie.

"Ma'am, I won't ask again. Step. Back." He puffed out his chest as he maneuvered between her and Mason's body.

"I told you, the cops don't want you around their crime scene," Betty said. "I know what I'm talking about. I have plenty of experience."

The other woman said, "It's not a crime scene. He fell down the stairs. It's obvious."

"If that were the case, he wouldn't be lying on his face, now would he?" Betty whipped around and pinned Officer Hostas with a demanding look. "Tell her I'm right."

Hostas's fat lips flattened into a grim line, refusing to answer. But that didn't matter once Betty saw me making my way toward them.

"Cookie!" She waved at me. "We need to call Detective Hottie right away. Mason didn't fall down the stairs. He was pushed. Look at him."

I checked out Amazon Barbie first but didn't recognize her. She didn't look upset, but she didn't look scared or disturbed either. Almost as if this wasn't her first dead body. I looked behind Betty where Mason was sprawled, face down, at the bottom of the stairs. She wasn't off on the mannequin description.

This would take delicate handling. With

59

the slightest hint that a crime had been committed, Betty would insist on "helping."

I cleared my throat. "You don't know for a fact he was pushed . . . unless you witnessed it."

"Of course I didn't see it. Duh! But I've watched enough of those cop shows to know that when people slip and fall down the stairs, they land on their backside. I've got twenty bucks that says he got pushed."

I hated to admit it, but Betty had an excellent point. I looked at Hostas and shrugged. He sighed in a way that sounded familiar — reminiscent of Homicide Detective Malone when he had had his fill of our unwanted theories.

"What do you think?" I probed.

"I have my suspicions. I've already called Malone. He's on his way."

I took that for the fair warning it was. "Then this is a good time for us to get out of here. Come on, Betty, let's go."

"I don't want to miss seeing my future boyfriend. Besides I'm sure he's going to want to ask me questions." She pulled a compact mirror from her straw handbag and checked her hair and strawberry-red eyebrows.

Oh, yes, he'd absolutely want to ask her questions. Probably along the lines of, "Why are you here? Do I need to arrest you or simply toss you in jail?" In Betty's world, the only question the detective was interested in asking her was where she wanted to go for their first date.

I was finally getting along with Detective Malone. If Mason's death turned out not to be an accident, the last thing I wanted was to stick my nose in his business . . . and homicide was his business.

I eyed Hostas. "If you've already called Malone, do you want Betty to stay here so he can question her or would you rather we wait for him at the shop?"

Betty smiled seductively as she slipped closer to him. "Don't you worry, Good-looking. I'll stay out of the way. I'll wait right over there by those Prada purses while you look at that paper Mason is clutching in his left hand."

We all turned and looked at the scrap of paper in his awkwardly clenched fist. I won't lie; I was curious as to what, if anything, was jotted on the paper. I could make out a few numbers: five . . . seven . . . and possibly a nine.

"They know how to do their job. Has anyone told Quinn?" I asked Officer Hostas.

He reluctantly pulled his attention away

from studying Mason. "Who's Quinn?"

"His wife. Yesterday she mentioned she had an appointment at the spa this morning, but I don't know which one."

Betty scoffed. "That's convenient."

I elbowed her. "Stop."

"Well it is," she insisted. "We've solved plenty of murders to know the first suspect is always the spouse. Someone needs to drag her bony behind downtown and give her the third degree."

" 'Someone' is not us. And if we were investigating, we'd start with Amazon Barbie. She's the one you found hunched over Mason." *Sheesh!* I had just said we needed to stay out of it, but the first line of questioning was so obvious, I couldn't stop myself.

At the mention of Amazon Barbie we all realized she had disappeared at some point. How had we not noticed?

Betty pulled out a notebook from her handbag. "Oh, good point. We need to track her down. She's giant-sized so she should be pretty easy to find. Have you thought about getting a PI license, Cookie? We could do it together."

"No," Officer Hostas and I said simultaneously.

I glared at him. "No need to be rude."

"Sorry," he muttered.

I sighed. "Put your notepad away. We're leaving this to the professsionals."

"Sheesh. They're only professionals because they get paid. I could get paid, too. I'm good at investigations. I'm even better at undercover jobs. I know how to blend in to the crowd."

I choked back my disbelief at the claim coming from the woman who stood before us in bright-purple silky loungewear, pearls, and white running shoes.

"You wouldn't know how to blend in if you were invited to a pajama party," Hostas muttered under his breath.

What he said.

This wasn't how I imagined my day would begin. Coffee at nine a.m. Check. A friendly chat with my best friend at nine fifteen. Check. Drag Betty away from a possible crime scene at nine forty-five. Nope, that wasn't top of mind.

We managed to open the shop by eleven, believe it or not, regular business hours. In the hour we'd been open, a number of loyal customers had already stopped by. Unfortunately, they weren't interested in purchasing anything. They all wanted the latest gossip. Betty had worked her magic and managed to convince two of them to purchase a bottle of pawlish and a couple of bags of gourmet dog treats.

My stomach growled. I realized in all the activity this morning, I never ate breakfast. I still needed to tell Betty and Grey about my trip home.

"Cookie, pay attention. I'm talking to you." Betty snapped her thin fingers inches from my face.

I backed away from Betty before she accidently poked me in the eye. "Sorry, I was thinking about lunch. I never asked you. Did you recognize the blond woman at the Reeds' shop?" I asked, straightening the interactive toys.

"Amazon Barbie? No. I'd remember her. She's a *big* girl."

I silently agreed. About her being memorable. "I wonder who she is." Her demeanor was noteworthy to me. The first time I'd found a dead body, I was a mess. She didn't seem to be bothered.

"Earth to Cookie!" Betty sighed. "Did you hear me tell ya about the treat jars?"

"What about treat jars?"

"I ordered some new ones a couple of weeks ago. The shipment should arrive today."

"How many?" I asked, not really sure I was ready to hear the answer.

"Ladies," a slick male voice greeted us.

We were so engrossed in our conversation that neither of us heard the doorbell chime.

Callum MacAvoy, local TV reporter for *Channel 5 News* stood in front of us with his TV-ready grin and annoying LA charm. Not only was he thirsty for fame, he was a pain in my backside.

"Hubba hubba." Betty wiggled her eyebrows. "Nice sports jacket."

Ugh. I wasn't as impressed with him or his wardrobe choice of a purple plaid shirt and gray tweed jacket as horndog Betty was. It was supposed to hit eighty-four degrees today. The jacket was excessive.

I met him in front of the rhinestone dog bowls in an attempt to keep him from getting too far into the shop. "Is there something I can do for you, MacAvoy?"

He didn't have a dog. He didn't have a girlfriend who had a dog. And Bow Wow had not been broken into. That left the movie festival or Mason's accidental death. For someone whose main motivation in life was to advance his career, his focus would be the latter.

"It's good to see you, too, Melinda. I heard you're working on the movie festival for next month."

I wasn't buying his attempt at social niceties for a second. "You're leading with a fluff piece? Next you'll tell me you're tracking society weddings at the Montage."

He shot us a confident grin as he bypassed me and headed straight for Betty who stood behind the counter. "I can investigate multiple stories at once. I'm a talented guy."

I wanted to roll my eyes in exasperation, but I was afraid they might stick to the back of my head. His talent was overly exaggerated.

He leaned against the counter attempting to project an air of trusted charm. "Since you brought it up," he continued, undeterred by my annoyed silence, "have you heard anything new about the break-ins?"

"No."

Betty zipped around the counter and shuffled up next to him. "Why don't you ask me a question, Lover Boy?"

He hesitated, looking a tad nervous. He returned his attention to me. "You answered rather quickly. Would you like to take a second to think about it?"

"Not really." I pushed past him and moved to the opposite side of the counter.

"Is there something you don't want me to know?" he asked.

"You have quite the imagination." I grabbed a spray bottle of surface cleaner and a rag, and proceeded to wipe down the counter top.

"Cleaning up Hot Stuff's cooties?" Betty quipped.

Something like that.

"MacAvoy, haven't you learned by now that if you want to know something, just ask me." I probably wouldn't answer, but I'd respect him more if he was straightforward and not couch his questions in a manipulative manner.

"Is that a yes? On the record?" He pulled out a voice recorder from his jacket pocket and shoved it under my nose.

When he was this annoying there was only one way to get rid of him.

"Oh, definitely." A soft seductive smile teased the corners of my mouth. I leaned in and spoke clearly into the mini microphone. "I am not a police officer. I have no idea what direction the investigation is headed. And Callum MacAvoy is at his best when reporting on society fluff pieces. I wish he'd do more."

He shut off the recorder. "That was unnecessary."

Betty cackled. "She got you."

I tossed the cloth and bottle back under the counter. "Why are you here? Don't you have an inside track or informant at the police station like all the other reporters?"

"Never said I didn't." He flashed a devil-ish smile. "I heard the police had a sketch of the Bash 'n Dash suspect."

I couldn't keep the surprise off my face.

"I guess I know something you don't," he taunted.

I narrowed my eyes. It was hard to tell if he was lying. Not that it mattered, he was right; I had no idea they had a sketch, let alone a suspect. But like I'd told him, I wasn't a cop so it wasn't as if I was failing at my job.

"Do you know who gave the description?" I asked. I knew I should have dropped it. But darn, as much as I knew how to get his attention, he knew how to get mine. Plus, if they were close to solving the rash of break-ins, I'd feel comfortable to bring Missy back to the shop.

"Oh, so now you can have a conversation with me." He picked up a rhinestone collar and studied it. "You know, I've been in this weird little town for a couple of years now, and I still can't believe anyone would pay seventy dollars for this."

I gently took the collar out of his hand and returned it to the display case on the counter. "And that is why you are still considered an outsider. You of all people

68

should know there are more dogs here than there are children. And for some of us, our pets are our children. Once you understand that, and learn to appreciate it, you might be accepted into the community."

He studied me with a serious expression. "You're really into this."

"Into what? My business? Of course."

"I'll take it under advisement. What do you know about Mason Reed?"

I felt my heart skip a beat. He'd done a great job of getting me to drop my guard. Darn him. He wasn't here about the break-ins; that was just an ice-breaker for the real scoop snooping. "The same as you. He owns Hot Handbags with his wife Quinn."

"What else can you tell me about him? Is he a difficult neighbor? Is he easy to get along with? Did anyone have it out for him?"

I knew from experience that if there was a murder investigation, Malone did not talk about it. Especially to the media. If he didn't already know Mason was dead, I didn't want to tip him that it was possible his death could be something more than an accident.

"He's not a big talker. And he's not someone who is engaged in the business community so I can't give you too much on him. Why do you ask?"

"Well according to my contact at the police station . . ." He stared at me for a moment, making sure I understood he had an 'in.' "He's dead."

"Really?" I squeaked out. At this point I didn't know what he knew, and I was extremely aware I was talking to a reporter. As far as I knew only Betty was convinced he was pushed down the staircase.

He frowned. "You don't seem surprised by the news."

"That's because I'm the one who found him, Smarty Pants." Betty sashayed closer. "I'd be happy to give you an exclusive."

My shush to Betty fell on deaf ears.

"I don't think that's a good idea." I shook my head. Betty ignored me.

"Are you up for it?" She batted her eyes in Mr. TV's direction.

He swallowed hard. "On camera?"

"Of course. As you know, I'm excellent on TV. But I'll have to clear it with that hottie, Detective Malone."

I let out a pent-up breath. Maybe Betty had learned a few things the past couple of years.

Mason returned his attention to me. "Word on the street is he argued with your fiancé about a bad art deal."

"Grey would never negotiate a bad art

deal for anyone. Secondly, he's not my fiancé, and you know that. You're being obstinate."

He scoffed. "Still defending him to the death even after he dumped you. I don't understand your blind allegiance."

"Lookie here, Buster." Betty poked him in the chest. "Just because Mason picked a fight with Grey in our shop, doesn't mean Grey had anything to do with Mason's death. And it was Cookie who did the dumping."

I closed my eyes and let out a frustrated sigh. She couldn't help herself. I looked at MacAvoy who was all ears at Betty's juicy tidbits.

"So they argued? Are you suggesting Mason's death wasn't an accident, that he was murdered?" He turned an excited expression in my direction. "By that arrogant ex of yours?" He pulled out a notepad from the inner pocket of his jacket and scribbled away.

My blood pressure soared. "Of course not. If you're here to get dirt on Grey, you can turn right around and leave."

The front door opened again. We all turned to see Grey step inside looking casual, at least for him — dress slacks, crisp white shirt, sans suit jacket. Immediately his eyes darted around the room taking in the scene, assessing the situation. Sometimes he had the worst timing; other times he had the best timing. Today his timing couldn't be more alarming.

"MacAvoy." His greeting held a deceivingly dismissive tone.

Grey's intimidating gait was impressive. I wouldn't want to be on the receiving end of it. I had to give it to MacAvoy. He didn't flinch. At least not outwardly.

The TV reporter squared his shoulders. "Donovan. Anything you'd like to say, on the record of course?"

"No." My ex-fiancé had pulled out his tried-and-true one-word answer. We were on our way to a word-boxing match.

"You're back." Betty bounced on the toes of her white sneakers. She pointed her thumb toward MacAvoy. "He was trying to get information out of us, but we're steel traps." She pretended to zip her lips.

I coughed, hiding my laughter. Betty's imaginary zipper couldn't hold tight for five seconds. "MacAvoy was just leaving."

"I don't think I was." He faced Grey. "Ms. Foxx said you had an argument with Mason Reed and now he's dead. Are you a suspect?"

Grey looked at me. "What's he talking about?"

"Mason Reed really is dead. At first glance it looks like he fell down the stairs."

"First glance?"

"He was pushed," Betty chimed in.

I could see the questions piling up in Grey's head. I pulled him aside, keeping my back to our unwanted audience. My palms were sweaty. I kept my voice low. "It's possible Betty is on to something. When you fall down the stairs you don't land face first."

Grey's face was unreadable. "Not typically." He looked over my shoulder at Betty. "How do you know this?"

I followed his gaze to where Betty and MacAvoy stood, eavesdropping on our conversation.

Betty puffed her chest out, proud as a peacock. "I found him. Deader than a doornail."

MacAvoy flashed his condescending TV smile in our direction. "I file the story in a few hours. If you change your mind about the interview, you know where to find me."

"Don't hold your breath," Grey said.

I sighed in relief when Mr. TV walked out the door.

Betty sauntered up to Grey, and slipped

73

her thin arm through his. "He's a sexy guy, but a royal pain in the butt. Don't you worry. Cookie and I have your back."

He patted her hand. "Thanks, Betty, but you don't need to worry yourself about it."

I studied the rugged handsome face I knew so well. The look in his eyes said we did need to worry. My ex-fiancé's under-cover business was about to wreak havoc on my personal life.

CHAPTER FOUR

Grey had followed MacAvoy out the door without ever explaining why he'd stopped by in the first place. Had Grey not rushed off in the opposite direction of MacAvoy, I'd have worried Grey had changed his mind about the in-depth interview. And not in a good way.

Due to Grey's abrupt departure, I didn't have a chance to mention my trip and my win-win arrangement. Not that I'd have to convince him, in the end he was getting what he wanted. I shot him a quick text asking him to come back to the shop when he had a few minutes.

Business was brisk, and the afternoon passed by in a blur. As promised, Nina Fernandez and puppy Dash stopped by to try on his costume. He looked adorable in his black tux, red rose pin, and fake mustache. He was fixated with eating the mustache, so she bought two extra. His energetic puppy prance didn't channel "intimidating mob-ster," but it wouldn't matter, he would be a guaranteed show stopper on the Mobster Film Festival red carpet next month.

I was still undecided on what Missy should wear. The obvious female mobster costume was a wedding dress, but I wasn't known for doing what was expected. I leaned toward Bonnie and Clyde (Missy as Bonnie, me as Clyde) or even prisoner uniforms. Oh, Mama would skin me alive if she even knew I was considering dressing as an inmate, knowing my photo would be taken. Of course, that just made it all the more enticing.

Nina and Dash left with a promise to see us at the festival, if not sooner. While I was helping a new customer decide on a collar and leash ensemble, Betty's order of porcelain treat jars arrived. All fifty jars.

She assured me she had ordered only ten containers. Too bad she hadn't read the whole description — five jars to a box. I had no idea how long it would take to sell the lot. I made a mental note to tell Grey only he could place special orders and to keep Betty away from the computer.

I sent her to the storage room to unpack and price the new merchandise. The sooner the jars were on the floor, the sooner we'd move them out the door. Betty vowed to sell them all by Christmas. Her heart was in the right place, but the jars would likely come to the same fate as the dog sweaters. Maybe we could have a buy-a-treat-jar-get-a-dog-sweater-for-free sale.

It was time to take away Betty's purchasing privileges. How did you tell an eighty-something-year-old she was grounded? Surely, parenting a teenager was easier than dealing with my favorite senior citizen.

While Betty was in the back, I turned my attention to the Mobster Film Festival, which was only five weeks away. I was short five thousand dollars of the Paws for Angels's sponsorship goal. Although, with Mason dead, it was possible I was ten thousand behind if Quinn decided she didn't want to, in her words, "clean up Mason's mess." I wasn't even sure what that meant.

I wish I'd listened closer to Mama when she was blabbering about the appropriate length of time to pass before approaching a new widow regarding volunteering and begging for charitable donations, but I had been fourteen and more interested in barrel racing than learning my role in Dallas society.

I was jotting down a new list of possible

sponsors when Luis and his pudgy, long-haired dachshund, Barney, waddled into the shop.

I greeted them as they made their way toward me. "Hey there. Two of my favorite customers. Barney's looking good."

Barney had had a weight problem since I'd known him. Dr. Darling, local veterinarian and good friend, had convinced Luis to put Barney on a strict diet and exercise program. It was working. The lovable pooch had lost a significant amount of weight over the past few months. Luis, on the other hand, seemed to be gaining whatever Barney had lost.

"Thanks, Mel." He looked around, rubbing his new double chin. "Is Betty in today?"

"She's in the back." Luis liked to dress his dog in costumes. Today he had dressed the dog like a purple jumbo crayon. The perfect outfit for the chubby doxie. I came out from behind the counter. I bent down and scratched Barney behind the ear. I really wanted to give him a treat, but I was pretty sure that wasn't on his doggie menu. "Is there something I can help you with?"

"She placed a special order for us."

Barney sighed and stretched out next to Luis's feet.

Lord, please tell me it was for a treat jar.

"I don't recall seeing anything come in with your name on, but that doesn't mean it's not here. I'll take a look in the back. What did you order?"

"No, no. That's okay." He stopped me with a sharp shake of his head. He cleared his throat. "Word around town is Betty found Mason Reed dead." He spoke softly as if sharing a dark family secret.

He wasn't just here to pick up a special order; he was shopping for gossip.

"News travels fast."

"Sure. Do you think his murder had anything to do with the break-ins?"

"No one said anything about murder. How about we let Detective Malone do his job?"

He perked up. "If it's not a murder, why's the homicide guy involved?"

Geez. Good question. I wasn't doing a very good job of tamping down a murder rumor. "Honestly, we don't know. But if he is, you know Malone; he's a thorough kinda guy." It was a weak explanation, and we both knew it.

"I thought I heard your voice." Betty shuffled her way toward us holding a brown cardboard box. "I got your special order, Luis. Did you hear I found another dead

79

guy? I'm on a roll."

He avoided making eye contact with me and instead focused on Betty. "I heard he broke his neck."

I sighed. The dead body gossip train had left the station. History had proven that once it had departed, it was impossible to stop, especially with Betty as the conductor.

"He was sprawled out like a shattered stick figure. Never thought a body could bend like that. I would have taken a picture, but I didn't think about it. Maybe next time."

Good grief. Next time? Time to derail the train. "Luis, we just got in a brand-new shipment of treat jars. Maybe you'd like to look at one?"

Betty snickered. "She doesn't want us talking about the investigation. I'm thinking about getting my PI license. You'd hire me, right, Luis?"

"Sure. Not sure what for, but if I needed an investigator, I'd hire you and Mel."

"Not Cookie, just me."

He looked between us, panicked indecision written on his face. "Oh, well . . . uh, sure. Probably. Maybe."

Offended, Betty dropped his box on the counter. "You'll change your mind once you need me. Maybe to find your lost dog."

Barney was sawing logs. The only running he was doing was in his dreams.

"By the way, I still think you should've bought the one with the skull and cross-bones. This one is wimpy." Betty handed him the box.

"Barney is more of a Mohawk kind of guy."

We all looked at Barney. His serious dark eyes and tubby belly straining against his purple crayon costume didn't shout "born to be wild." More like "born to snarf dog treats."

"What exactly did you order?" I asked.

"A motorcycle helmet."

Luis was an average-looking guy, a little on the shy side. I'd never pegged him for someone who desired freedom and adventure of the road.

"I didn't realize you rode. What type of bike do you have?"

He shook his head. "I don't. It's for a costume I'm putting together."

Of course. What was I thinking? "You must be getting ready for the Paws for Angels's fundraiser next month."

His lips split into a fat grin. "Oh, yes. Did I ever tell you Barney had been trained to be a service dog?"

Betty and I looked at each other. I'm sure

she was thinking the same thing I was. *Barney?* Don't get me wrong, dog breeds other than the traditional Labradors, Golden Retrievers, and German Shepherds could be trained to perform specific tasks for their owners, but a wiener dog dressed up like someone's kid for Halloween?

Luis took our silence as an invitation to continue, which it was. I was dying to hear the rest of the story and learn about Barney's hidden talents other than winning the local wiener race. (How Barney managed to win a Dachshund race was a whole other story.)

"He's a true lap dog. Loves people —"

"And loves naps," Betty interrupted.

Luis blushed. "Anyway, we were all set to begin companion hospital visits, but we found out he's allergic to bleach." He lowered his head to stare adoringly at his dachshund. "There's a lot of bleach fumes in a hospital. He sneezed and coughed for days after our initial visit. Doc Darling said Barney needed to retire before he developed tremors or seizures."

That seemed extreme, but I wasn't a vet, so who was I second guess the diagnosis?

"Are you sure he's not allergic to all the dog cologne you spray on him?" Betty asked.

Luis liked purchasing dog cologne the same way Betty liked selling pawlish — they were *obsessed.* I had to agree with Betty; normally, Barney's cologne was overpowering. Today, it wasn't bad.

Luis's face reddened. "I took your advice and only squirt him three times now."

"That's better than bathing him in it. I bet his dandruff has improved."

I glared at Betty to stop harassing poor Luis.

"You're doing a great job with his cologne," I encouraged him.

Luis ducked his head. "Thanks."

"I have a question. Don't you mean Barney was training to be a therapy dog?" I asked.

Luis was confused about the differences between a service dog and a therapy dog. He wasn't alone. Since working with Paws for Angels, I learned that was the number-one misunderstanding. A service dog has been specially trained for their owner's disability. Such as opening and closing doors, diabetic seizure alerts, mobility help, pushing elevator buttons, or turning lights on and off. Barney was a little short to reach the light switch.

Luis tilted his head and pursed his lips. "It's all the same. Isn't it?"

I smiled gently. I didn't want to hurt his feelings or embarrass him. "No. If Barney was a service dog, he wouldn't belong to you anymore. He'd live with the person he was helping. A therapy dog is a pet that's trained to help other people become healthier. Like visiting hospital patients to cheer them up."

"Oh, no. I would never give Barney away. I don't know what I'd do without my little buddy." Luis's eyes welled with unshed tears as he thought about being separated from his beloved pooch.

Before I had to wrangle up a large amount of false sympathy to comfort a guy who was imagining losing his dog over a situation that never happened, the front doorbell jingled announcing a new customer. It was Grey.

"Hey, Handsome." Betty immediately waved him over. "Did you forget something?" She batted her eyes in his direction. "Or should I say someone?" She nudged me aside to reach him, not that it had been a competition.

"The boss lady requested my presence." His smile didn't reach his eyes. I was immediately on alert.

"Ha. That's a good name for you." Betty elbowed me as she laughed.

Grey gave her his customary quick peck on the cheek before turning to me. "Can we talk in your office?" He sounded tired.

Betty rubbed her hands together. "I've got the store. You and Grey kiss and make up. Take your time."

I sighed. "There's no kissing."

Luis looked uncomfortable. Betty disappointed. Grey kept his emotions under wraps like a good G-man.

"When did you become so boring?" Betty asked.

"She's not talking to me," Grey denied.

I shook my head. "You're not helping. Betty, ring up Luis's helmet. Then organize the bandanas and make sure the clearance items have been tagged correctly. And *don't* order anything."

"Blah, blah, blah. Slave driver." Betty walked to the register. "Whaddya say, Luis? Can I interest you in one of our new treat jars? We only have a handful. I expect them to go really fast. You can be the first to buy one, be the trend setter."

"I don't know. I think I'll just take the helmet."

"Let me show it to you before you make up your mind," she pressed.

Grey chuckled as we headed toward my office. "Always the saleswoman."

"She's got fifty of them to sell by Christmas."

Grey whistled softly.

"If you know what's good for you, you'll purchase two before you leave today. Give them away as Christmas gifts." I closed the door behind us once we were inside my office. "Thanks for stopping by."

He shoved his hands in the pockets of his trousers. "I'll admit I was surprised to get your text."

"Thought I deleted your number?" I joked.

"After our last conversation, it had crossed my mind." He looked subdued.

I was curious about his abrupt departure earlier. More importantly, I wanted to know where he went and if the errand was case related.

"You left in a hurry this morning." I tucked a lock of hair behind my ear.

"Something came up."

More like someone came up dead.

Our conversation was strained. I felt like I was trying to find my way around in an unfamiliar dark room. There was no point pursuing the reason for his abrupt departure, so I moved on to why I had asked him to stop by. I took a deep breath and jumped in feet first.

"I've given some thought to your request, and I think we might be able to come to an agreement that works for both of us."

A spark of interest flashed across his face. His tired eyes brightened. "I'm listening."

I leaned against the edge of the wooden table I used as a desk. "Mitch and Nikki became parents to a baby girl. Elmsly Tillie."

"That's great news. Congratulations to them." Grey's face softened. He leaned against the table next to me, side by side. "You'll make a wonderful aunt."

My heart melted at his understanding of how much I already loved my niece. "They're coming home, to Dallas, at the end of the month, and I told Mama I'd come home, too."

His face closed off. "I see."

"I was thinking that while I was gone, you could keep an eye on Betty and the shop."

"A cover," he said simply.

His reaction confused me. Wasn't this what he wanted? "It's what you asked for."

We studied each other in heavy silence. Grey's cell rang, cutting through the tension. I jumped, startled. Almost reluctantly, he quickly checked the number. He frowned. I couldn't tell if his reaction was because he recognized the number or not. Ignoring the call, he slipped the phone back in his jacket.

"You can take that." I pushed off the desk to leave. Grey grabbed my arm to stop me.

"My investigation has already started. Do you mind if I come back tomorrow?"

"Any chance your argument with Mason has anything to do with your case and why you're so eager to start? Or that phone call you're ignoring? Or why you look so tired?" I didn't think he'd actually tell me, but he knew I'd ask, and I hated to disappoint either of us.

He released my arm but remained silent. No elaboration. No details.

"You can't blame a girl for asking." My heart was heavy. Nothing had changed between us for the better. From the look on his face, I knew deep down he felt the same. "Look, start whenever you want, today, tomorrow, next week. Whatever works. But you can't tell people we're dating or that we're getting back together. I won't lie about that. It affects too many people."

"I've always respected your integrity."

I've always respected your integrity? Hogwash. I couldn't think of a time he'd ever sounded more like a fed than right now. Whatever sentimental emotion I had been feeling was now squashed.

I squinted at him to ensure my irritation

with him was clearly visible. "While I'm gone, keep an eye on Betty. She seems to stumble over trouble without trying."

"She's not the only one."

His attempt to lighten the mood fell flat.

"Can you keep an eye on Betty and conduct your super-secret investigation at the same time?" Gosh I knew I sounded awful, but I couldn't stop myself. Honestly, it wasn't that I begrudged his undercover work; it was that he hid behind it.

"I can't promise to be her babysitter, but if you're asking me to make sure she doesn't burn down the store or buy out the pawlish manufacturers, I can do that."

"Get her to sell those treat containers." I walked to the door. I grabbed the doorknob then paused. "There's one more stipulation," I said over my shoulder.

He raised a brow. "Just one?"

"This is a deal breaker. If I feel like your investigation hampers my business, I get to pull the plug on your operation."

He stood. "Melinda, I can't tell you what I'm investigating, but you know I would never put you, Betty, or your business in jeopardy."

I spun around and shoved my hands on my hips. "Let's be honest. For the past two years, you've done everything in your power to keep your 'work' as far from me as possible."

"For good reason."

"Yes, yes. The 'undercover' part. But look at this from my point of view. You show up on my doorstep and suddenly you want those two worlds to collide. I can't help but feel there's more going on then you're letting on. I can't help but ask questions. It's who I am, and you know that."

He remained silent.

"So we're good?"

"Once I start this, I can't just stop. This would be official. It's not personal."

"And if I have to kick you out of my shop, remember it's not personal." I released a deep breath, collecting my nerves and trying to calm myself. "How long do you think this will take?"

"Hopefully a few weeks. With any luck, we'll close the case by the time you get back."

"And then we'll go back to normal." Whatever the heck that meant.

"Right." Was it me or did he look unhappy about that? I searched his face closer, but whatever I thought I'd seen was gone.

"Okay." I held out my hand. "Deal."

He shot me an amused grin, catching me off guard.

"We're shaking?" he asked. "That's not how we've sealed our agreements in the past."

Why was he insisting on bringing up the past? I raised my eyebrows. "Well, that's how it's happening today."

He shook my hand. "Deal."

"Now that we've settled the business portion of our conversation, I have one more question," I said.

He chuckled. "You're full of questions today. Shoot."

"Is there really a problem with the electricity at the gallery?"

The sexy mischievous smile I had loved so much made an appearance. "Of course."

It was the way he said it that I knew it was all part of the cover. I couldn't help it; I returned his smile. Lordy, what had I gotten myself and Betty into?

I opened the office door. "Brace yourself. Once Betty knows you're sticking around, she's going to be full of questions and fawn all over you."

"I can't wait."

CHAPTER FIVE

Betty was over the moon; she and Grey would be working together, without me, for a whole week. She immediately began to make plans, herding Grey around the shop like an excited Australian Shepherd. The arrangements were hush-hush. I shuddered thinking about all the chaos she was planning to unleash on Grey. He might have met his match. On the other hand, I got a kick thinking about Grey trying to keep an oblivious Betty out of his investigation. I wasn't sure he'd thought that through before he agreed to my plan.

It was almost three, and I was starving. Betty offered to grab lunch for all three of us — her way to make sure Grey stuck around. She promised to be quick. In Betty time, that meant we had at least forty-five minutes before we'd see her or food.

Grey asked that I give him thirty minutes and tucked himself away in the office with the door closed. I had no idea what he was doing, but I was certain it had to do with his investigation. I focused on reviewing the clearance merchandise Betty hadn't finished pricing.

I had just wrapped up marking down the bandanas (Betty had barely made a dent in the pile) when a rather good-looking man with an equally good-looking Golden Retriever walked into the shop.

"Hi, can I help you find something?" I asked.

He smoothed his tousled sandy-blond hair. "You must be Melinda. I'm Colin. Darby's . . . er . . . friend." He crossed the shop in my direction with an outstretched hand.

"It's nice to meet you." I shook his hand. Firm grip, but not overpowering. I was relieved it wasn't limp and sweaty.

He wasn't what I was expecting. The way Darby had talked about him, I'd pictured a softer look, almost an intelligent nerdy type who liked chick flicks and sappy greeting cards. Not a tousled heartthrob who could easily book a catwalk gig for Abercrombie and Fitch. Good for Darby.

"This is Goose." He patted the Golden's head that stood next to him.

"Hi, boy." I held my hand out for him to

sniff. He lavished a handful of doggie kisses to the back of my hand then left me to explore the store.

Colin's dreamy brown eyes appraised me and then the shop. "Nice variety of items."

"Thanks. Darby has spoken very highly about you. She thinks you're almost as good with animals as my lovely cousin Caro."

Bryan Goosling (I still think that's the best dog name ever), aka Goose, wagged his solid body as he shoved his face into the basket of toys sitting on the floor. Colin snapped his fingers, and the dog immediately stopped sniffing and returned to stand next to his owner.

Colin gave me an uncertain smile as he continued our inquest of each other. "Darby is extremely supportive. I, ah, haven't had the opportunity to meet Caro, but she has an excellent reputation around town as a pet behaviorist."

A non-answer about Caro. Hard to tell if he really knew anything about her or if he was attempting to get on my good side. Either way, he wasn't aware that Caro and I weren't on face-to-face speaking terms.

"How did you and Darby meet?" I asked.

He cocked his head and looked surprised. "Darby hasn't told you?"

"Sure she has. I'd just like to hear your

version of the story." I was Darby's best friend. He had to know if I ever got him alone, I'd interrogate him.

"Oh." He cleared his throat. "Well, being relatively new to town, a friend —" He paused for a minute. "You probably want to know which friend."

I shrugged. "I am curious." I already knew, but I was all about comparing notes.

"Jade from Divine Dog Spa."

Jade had an appetite for drama and gossip. She was also infamous for her successful doggie matchmaking. It had only been a matter of time before she'd turned her "talents" toward people.

"So Jade set up the blind date?"

"It took some convincing, but Jade finally got Darby to agree."

"It's the British accent."

He smiled in agreement. "Jade was right. Darby is beautiful inside and out."

"Yes, she is. Many people would do anything for her."

"Indeed. She does seem to inspire people to be at their best."

"I wouldn't be fulfilling my best friend duty if I didn't tell you that if you ever deliberately hurt her or if I find out you're hiding some huge secret like a wife and three kids, you're into polygamy, or you are a serial killer, you will answer to me."

He blinked a few times, digesting my best friend speech.

I patted him on the arm. "Don't worry, I'm not really that scary."

It took him a second to catch up to my change in topics. He released a tense laugh, while adjusting the collar of his dark-blue polo shirt. "Darby said you were a straight shooter. She wasn't kidding."

"I have my faults, but not having the backs of the people closest to me isn't one."

I couldn't tell if his nervous energy was due to apprehension or anxiety. If he was really as successful as Darby claimed, there was more to him than met the eye. Maybe I could get Grey to run a background check on him, just to be on the safe side.

"Goose seems like a great dog. How long have you had him?"

The Golden had gotten bored and returned to nosing around the basket of toys. Colin held his hand, palm down, and Goose immediately sat. His fluffy tail playfully smacked the floor in an infectious rhythm. I couldn't help but share his goofy smile.

"He's been my wingman since he was a pup. We've been through a lot together." Colin's brown eyes turned serious as if momentarily transported back in time. And from the darkness in his eyes, it seemed the past wasn't full of puppies and rainbows. Evil unicorns were a possibility.

I stopped myself from snapping him out of it and let him work through his memories. When he looked at me, he seemed to have returned to the present.

"So did Darby fill you in about Missy? I'm assuming that's why you stopped by," I said.

He nodded. "She said Missy is suffering from separation anxiety."

"She chewed up my favorite motorcycle boots. She charges outside when I come home trying to escape."

"And this just started?"

I nodded. "It's been going on for a few weeks."

Goose scooted closer to me, begging to be acknowledged and adored. I lowered my hand and let him sniff it. After a quick nuzzle, I stroked his back and scratched behind his ears.

"Darby suggested I talk to you about spending time with her, letting her outside, and maybe taking her for a walk."

He tilted his head, concentrating on my answers. "What about cuddle time?"

I blinked in confusion. "Cuddle time?" I repeated like an idiot.

97

"If you're interested or feel that's missing, I can make time for it."

"You schedule cuddle time?"

"Absolutely. Cuddling is crucial for a deep relationship. It promotes bonding, reduces stress and social anxiety."

He knew how to hook a true pet lover. "How long do you normally cuddle for?"

"That depends on the client. Typically, anywhere from ten minutes to an hour."

Good grief. I hope he didn't charge Darby for cuddling. I noticed Grey standing quietly in the background, listening to our conversation.

"You might as well join us," I said.

"Mel, I had no idea you were that lonely."

"Ha, ha." I made quick introductions between the two, explaining that Grey was learning the ropes so he could help Betty while I was out of town.

"Back to cuddling. I take it this is extra? You know, since we're setting aside a specific time for it." As ridiculous as the conversation sounded, he had me, and he knew it.

"Since you're a friend of Darby's, I'll give you the friends' and family rate of twenty dollars for thirty minutes." He smiled brightly, as if the discount made it all seem normal.

I never thought I'd pay for someone to sit

on the couch and cuddle Missy.

"Mel, that's a bargain." Grey's innocent smile wasn't fooling me. He was enjoying the absurdity of the conversation. Betty hadn't returned with our lunch yet; otherwise she'd be negotiating her own personal cuddling time with Darby's boyfriend.

"So how does this work?" I asked.

"I'd like to come over and meet Missy in her environment. See if we're a good fit."

I chuckled. "Missy likes everyone. If you're going to take her to the beach and feed her treats, she'll love you."

Undeterred by my conviction that Missy would adore him, he continued explaining his process. "Once we've established we're a good fit, I can start coming over. I'd also like to schedule a time for Missy to meet Goose. I like to take him with me whenever possible."

Goose smiled and licked the air hearing his name. I patted his head.

"The four of us could meet at the dog park. When can you meet Missy one on one?"

"I'm free tomorrow."

I nodded. "I can make that work." I turned to Grey. "Can you watch the shop with Betty?"

He smiled. "Wouldn't miss it for the world."

The front door opened, and in stalked Detective Judd Malone, six feet and some inches of unyielding law enforcement. His dark jeans, black shirt, and black leather jacket didn't alter that initial impression one iota. Dang. I swallowed hard, sending Grey serious side-eye. Hopefully, Malone was here to talk to Betty, who was conveniently out.

"Detective." I shot him my best nothing-to-see-over-here smile.

"Melinda." His poker-face expression was all business. He looked at Grey. "Donovan. I was told I might find you here."

"You found me." Grey might have sounded affable, but I recognized that look of stone-cold sober resistance and the flex in his jaw.

Malone's gaze bounced between Grey and me. I knew what he was thinking. It's what everyone thought when they saw the two of us together.

"No, we're not back on. Have you met Colin Sellers? Colin, this is Homicide Detective Malone. Laguna's finest."

Colin cleared his throat and smiled tentatively. "Ah, nice . . . ah, good, to meet you."

Malone had that effect on people. That

split second of mentally running through your entire life wondering if there was anything he could arrest you for.

Malone nodded and managed to get out a "Nice to meet you," before he turned his attention to Grey. "Got a minute?"

Grey looked at me. "Can we use your office?"

I tried my best to not look nervous, but my fake smile didn't stick. I didn't know why I was worried. Just because Grey and Mason had an argument in my store the day before Mason was found dead, had nothing to do with Malone looking for Grey. "Sure." My voice broke. "Help yourselves."

They headed to my office leaving me and Colin alone.

"Are you and the detective friends?" he asked.

"Er, I wouldn't say friends." I watched the office door close behind Grey. Nope, definitely not friends. Heck, we were approaching the *friendly* stage. You know, where I stopped poking my nose into his murder investigations, and he stopped threatening to throw me in jail.

"Oh, I thought I detected some type of familiarity between you."

"Because he called me by my first name?"
He nodded.

101

"Let's just say our paths have crossed a time or two."

"In a social setting?"

"Not exactly." I wished he would stop talking long enough for me to see if I could overhear the conversation in my office.

"You've needed him in a professional capacity?"

I shrugged. "That's one way to look at it."

"He's serious."

"As a heart attack. He's fair, but can also suffer from tunnel vision."

As eager as I was to grill Darby's new boyfriend, I wanted to hear what Malone was talking about with Grey more. I had a bad feeling this was one of those times Malone's single-mindedness could be a problem. It was time to switch gears and get rid of Colin. I could grill him about Darby another time.

I rubbed my hands together and smiled brightly. "So about you and Missy, let's do it."

He returned my smile. "That's great. I think I can help you both."

Wonderful. Now he sounded like Caro. *It's not the dog that needs to be trained, but the human.*

We agreed he'd come to my place at nine the next morning. He assured me it wouldn't take more than thirty minutes for the initial meeting, and I assured him I wasn't worried about the time. I rushed him and his happy-go-lucky Golden out the door before quietly making my way toward the office. I pressed myself against the wall and tiptoed toward the door.

At first I couldn't hear anything but muffled voices over my own nervous breathing.

I managed to even out my breaths in time to hear Grey say, "No." I grimaced. His tone was closed off and annoyed. This little confab was definitely not social in nature.

"So you . . ." mumble, mumble, mumble, "original and he," mumble, mumble, mumble, mumble. "You could tell this how?"

"It's my job."

"Where were you this morning between seven and ten?"

Crapola. I heard that question loud and clear.

"Home."

"Anyone with you?"

"No."

I had a sinking feeling in the pit of my stomach. Having been on the receiving end of a Malone questioning, I knew their conversation was not swinging in Grey's favor.

"When was the last time . . . ?" I didn't need to hear Malone finish that sentence. I was certain he'd asked about the last time Grey had talked to Mason.

I couldn't make out Grey's response, but it was short. Malone asked him another question, but again, I couldn't make out the words. I moved closer to the door and pressed my ear against the wall.

"Cookie, what are you doing?" Betty called out.

I jumped, whacking my head against the wall. I spun around and raced toward Betty before Malone and Grey opened the door to investigate the noise.

"Shh!"

Betty set a large bag of food on the counter. "Are we eavesdropping? Who's in there?" She wasn't very good at whispering.

"We are doing no such thing." My head was still spinning from hitting it against the wall. I motioned for her to stay at the counter, but she ignored me and headed in my direction. I blocked her path, keeping her from reaching the office door.

"I didn't hear you come in," I stalled.

"Kinda hard with your ear stuck to the door." She narrowed her eyes and glared up at me. "Who are we spying on?"

Before I could answer, the office door

swung open. Betty peered around me. She inhaled sharply as the men exited the office.

"I'll throw the sandwiches at them while you make a break for it."

"Just act normal." Once the words left my mouth I knew I'd said the wrong thing.

"Don't you worry. I got this." She pushed past me. "Detective, I've been meaning to hook up with you."

I swear I could hear Malone groan in dread. "Mrs. Foxx, I trust you're not harassing my officers."

"That's what I wanted to talk to you about. I'm thinking about getting my PI license."

Everyone froze.

"No," Malone ordered.

Grey's eyes widened, but he knew enough to stay silent.

Betty propped a hand on her hip. "I haven't even asked you my question."

"There's no need. The answer is still no."

"I need a recommendation," Betty continued to rattle on, undeterred. "And since I've helped you solve a number of murders recently, don't you think you owe me a small favor?"

Malone worked his jaw. I held my breath, worried he might just throw Betty in jail just to keep her off the streets.

"No," he snapped. "Donovan. Melinda." Without another word he brushed past Betty and me, and stalked out the front door.

"He'll come around." Betty grinned. "I haven't met a man yet who can say no to me."

CHAPTER SIX

For as long as I could remember, my mama had always told me most problems could be solved with a new lipstick or a "refresh" home project. Unlike my mama, I didn't enjoy major renovations in order to "freshen up" my home. That's what paint, curtains, and throw pillows were for. Since I loved my cozy home the way it was, I stopped by the drug store on the way home and picked up some lip gloss and a shea-and-coco-butter bath bomb.

I was dying to know what Malone and Grey had discussed. Grey had been closed-mouthed about the whole conversation other than saying Malone had asked the typical questions. And since I had been questioned by the homicide detective on more than one occasion, he said I knew how the conversation went. I didn't know why he felt the need to bring up my interrogation history with Malone. It wasn't as if La-

107

guna's first dead body had showed up after I moved to town a few years earlier.

Grey was correct. I knew Malone's standard investigation questions. What I didn't know was how Grey had answered. Since we weren't involved, I didn't feel I had the right to press. For now. One of the perks of him using my shop for surveillance was that there would be many more opportunities to ask him about it.

Missy was excited to see me. I loved her up and took her for a quick walk so she could take care of her business. Once we returned to the house, I whipped up a quick Mediterranean grilled cheese sandwich and poured myself a glass of pinot grigio.

I flipped on the television to keep Missy and me company as we cuddled on the couch — for free — and I ate dinner. The weather forecast was typical for this time of year, a high of mid-eighties, mostly sunny, with occasional morning fog.

When MacAvoy's tanned face and flashy white smile filled my screen, I choked on my sandwich.

"Cut back on the teeth whitening and fake tanning, Bud. You look like you've rolled in a bag a Cheetos," I told him through the television. He must have had a high school girl apply the thick veil of bronzer.

His listen-to-me-I'm-important announcer voice immediately set my teeth on edge. The piece he was reporting must have been the story he'd filed yesterday. True to his word, he referred to Grey without mentioning his name. He stated Mason had had a heated argument with a local art gallery owner the day before he died, which may or may not have anything to do with Mason's fall down the stairs. The police were still investigating and had not made an official determination yet, but had not ruled out foul play. If anyone had information, they were to notify the police.

I jumped up off the couch, startling Missy awake. She tumbled to the floor, then shook until her soft jowls jiggled. "You reckless news hack." I glared at the screen.

I tromped into the kitchen, then tossed my plate on the counter and watched it wobble toward the sink. With a sigh of frustration I refilled my wine glass. In the words of my Grandma Tillie, I was in a horn-tossing mood.

"I dare you to come back to my shop and ask me questions, MacAvoy."

A restless night's sleep didn't improve my mood. But a chai latte, passing marks from Colin Sellers, and a morning romp at the dog park with Missy made a decent start.

As we'd agreed, Colin had come by the house first to meet Missy at home. Missy had briefly sniffed Colin, experiencing him as any curious dog would. He had asked me to stay close but to not interact unless he instructed. For a second, he'd sounded as bossy as Caro. I didn't make him any promises. It had gone well enough that we moved to the dog park where his Golden Goose would join us.

The Bark Park, a couple of acres of fenced-in grass nestled in the Laguna Canyon, was as popular with humans as it was with their dogs. Once inside the double gate, Goose and Missy had greeted each other with the typical formal dog sniff. Within minutes, Goose had been distracted by a random tennis ball bouncing past us. Colin whistled for his Golden to return to our pack. The longer the four of us inter-acted as a group, the more tolerant the two dogs became of each other.

I watched Colin play with Missy and Goose. Colin's smile was just as goofy as his dog's. Missy, not being a lover of mind-lessly retrieving a ball without some type of food reward for more than a handful of minutes, found a bright patch of sunlight to stretch out and chill. In Missy's world, that translated into napping.

After inspecting the grass, ensuring it was free of doggie "presents," Colin had sweetly stretched out next to her, careful to never touch her, but letting her know he was there. After a couple of minutes she rolled to her back and presented her belly for a good rub. He'd won her over without offering her a treat. It was impressive. Of course, she was also a sucker for a good belly rub. Colin looked ridiculously pleased with himself. Missy was snoring.

We agreed he'd come to the house each afternoon to spend ninety minutes with Missy, starting that afternoon. Yes, that included cuddle time. I guess I was a sucker for anyone who wanted to treat my dog like their own.

Colin and Goose left to meet their next client, a Cavalier King Charles Spaniel who needed a morning potty break, a walk, and a hot breakfast of lamb and rice. Definitely sounded like the life fit for a king's loyal companion. Missy and I loaded up into the Jeep so I could take her home before I headed to the boutique.

As we pulled away from the Bark Park, my cell phone rang.

I pressed the hands-free button to answer. "Hello?"

"Melinda Langston? Evan Dodd." His voice was wobbly, tone uncertain. "I worked for Mason. As his bookkeeper."

"Oh, hello." I tightened my grip on the steering wheel, bracing for bad news.

"I have a check for you," he squeaked out.

"Really?"

"Let me clarify. It's for the charity Angels for Paws."

Well, Hell's Bells. Quinn was going to clean up Mason's mess after all. To be honest, I had expected she'd make me beg to get that check judging by her earlier comments. If I hadn't been driving down the Pacific Coast Highway, I'd have performed a happy dance.

At his suggestion, we agreed to meet at the Koffee Klatch an hour later. I assumed he wanted to meet there because Hot Handbags Boutique was still being processed by the crime scene team. That made me a wee bit anxious. If that were the case, then Mason probably hadn't fallen, but had been pushed down the stairs.

If true, Betty was right, and someone owed her twenty dollars. That in itself was alarming, but more importantly it explained Malone seeking out Grey for a "conversation." I told myself it meant nothing, but deep down I knew that was a lie. A "conversation" with Malone always meant something. Always.

I pulled in to my driveway and shut off the Jeep. Missy and I jumped out and hustled inside. I tossed her a couple of her favorite homemade paw print peanut butter snacks. She knew I was bribing her, but she was also a dog, so she inhaled the treats regardless, with only the tiniest of reproachful expressions. I left a note for Colin on the potty route Missy enjoyed the most and asked him to send me a couple of photos. Out of guilt, I set an additional two treats on a plate for Colin to give to Missy later that afternoon.

I hopped back in the Jeep and headed for the Koffee Klatch, my favorite coffee shop in town, to meet Evan. Once I had the check in hand, that would leave me only five thousand dollars to reach our donation goal.

I had contemplated asking Colin if he had a couple thousand he'd like to cough up. I was certain he'd be a sucker to support an organization that trained seizure response dogs, but he didn't strike me as the type with an overflowing bank account. Maybe it had been today's outfit of thrift store jeans, generic gray hoodie, and sneakers that had given off that impression. However, I knew a number of poorly dressed billionaires, so that impression was probably my fashion snobbery. Colin was a guy who was doing what he loved, not a slave to the almighty dollar. It was admirable. I understood Darby's attraction to him.

I arrived at the coffee shop and realized I had no idea what Evan Dodd looked like. While I waited in line to order, I glanced around the café looking for anyone I didn't recognize or who looked like a bookkeeper with a quivery voice.

Not exactly sure what a bookkeeper looked like, I didn't think the stereotypical image would have tattoo sleeves, look like a gym rat, or dress like a street performer. That left the six-foot-something, thin, curly-haired guy with glasses standing in the back of the shop who looked like he was about to bolt at the first sign of possible trouble.

My favorite barista, Verdi, was at the counter and had already called out my drink before I could order — just one of the perks of ordering the same drink for years. Verdi also worked for Caro as a receptionist. They'd had a few adventures of their own. I don't remember all the details, but I believe a while back, Caro had helped clear Verdi's brother of murder charges.

What can I say? Solving crime runs in the family.

I picked up my drink, left a generous tip for Verdi, and headed for my possible Evan at a table in the back. When I made eye contact with him, he nervously readjusted his round rimmed glasses, which were just a little too big for his face. Wouldn't I be embarrassed if the hunk in the white tank top with the rippling muscles was really a bookkeeper in disguise? Nah, I felt confident in my choice.

"Evan?" I asked, with a reassuring smile.

He nodded. "Melinda? Thanks for meeting me." He motioned for us to sit at the table.

I didn't want to be rude, but I didn't have an abundance of time to sit back and chat for an hour. Although for a five-grand donation, I'd take an hour coffee break if asked. He left me the chair with my back to the room, which made me uncomfortable. Grey had taught me well over the years to be aware of my surroundings. I dragged the chair around the table closer to Evan so I could see who was coming and going.

Evan's eyes widened, and he cleared his throat. "I — I have a girlfriend," he blurted.

I blinked. What an odd man. "Congratulations?"

He motioned between us. "You're sitting very close."

I smiled. "I don't like my back to the door. It's just a thing. Don't worry about it."

He didn't look one hundred percent convinced, but he dropped it. "Quinn says you're spearheading a donation drive for dogs, this Paws for Angels group."

I furrowed my brows. "Not exactly. I take it you haven't heard of the organization? They train response dogs, or assistance dogs, for people with seizures."

"Are they affiliated with the Animal Rescue League?"

"No. It's a separate organization, but there's a group of us who volunteer at the ARL who also support Paws for Angels. The organization needs to raise about fifty thousand dollars each year to cover costs since they don't charge their clients for the response dogs. The Laguna Mobster Film Festival event next month is a new fundraiser for them. The opening event is pet friendly. The theme is to bring your pooch dressed as your favorite mob character."

A quick smile peeked out. "That sounds like fun."

"You should purchase a ticket." He looked like a penny pincher, so I didn't mention the cost of a ticket was two hundred bucks a pop. "Do you have a dog?"

He shook his head. "No. I'm allergic."

I wasn't surprised. "There are a number of hypoallergenic breeds looking for forever homes. Terriers, Poodles, Bichon Frise, Chinese Crested —"

"Chinese Crested . . . those are hairless dogs?" He scrunched his face in disgust. "They look like alien pets."

"They're unique looking," I corrected. "And very emotionally attached to their humans." Probably a perfect choice for him.

He shifted in his chair. "I don't think my girlfriend would like one. How would you pet them? They don't have hair."

"You can still pet them. A dog's belly doesn't have hair, but you rub their belly anyway."

He looked confused. I changed the subject back to the reason we were meeting. "So you said you had a check for me?"

He quickly transformed from nerdy geek to confident, bookish geek. "I do. I wasn't convinced I should hand over such a large sum of money, but now that we've spoken, I think this donation is worthwhile. I will need a receipt with Paws and Angels —"

"Paws for Angels," I corrected. I sure hope he had the correct name on the check. I was losing confidence in Mason's book-keeper.

"Right. The receipt needs their Federal Identification Number."

"Of course. Once I give the check to the treasurer, she'll mail that to you."

He reached for a briefcase at his feet that I hadn't noticed until that moment and fished around inside. So much for being aware of my surroundings. He pulled out an envelope and held it in front of me without actually handing it to me. Almost as if he were taunting me with the donation, expecting me to perform a trick.

"Why does Quinn dislike you? You seem rather pleasant to me."

I did a double take. Quinn didn't like me? "You'd have to ask her."

All this time I had chalked up her chilly temperament and curt responses to her poor impression of a reality TV Laguna housewife. When all along it really was me she didn't like.

He made a face. "I have, uh, well sort of . . ." He cleared his throat. "I mean, she's not one to explain. She's closed mouth about such things."

Not that closed mouth if she'd blabbed to Evan about her dislike of me. And how discreet could Evan be if he was spilling client secrets to a stranger? I was finished talking about Quinn's inner circle. I plucked the check out of Evan's fingers before he stumbled upon a reason to keep it.

"Thank you."

"You're welcome." He adjusted his glasses again. "Ultimately, it's what Mason wanted."

"We appreciate that you honored his request." I opened the envelope to check the amount and name on the check. Seeing it was correct, I tucked the envelope inside my tote bag.

"Were you and Mason close?" I asked, taking the opportunity to learn more about who Mason really was.

"As close as anyone could be to him."

I took a sip of my chai. "What do you mean?"

He lowered his voice. "He was charming until he didn't get his way. Then he wasn't very easy to get along with. He had a rather child-like temper."

I scoffed. "I caught a glimpse of it. I had no idea he could fly off the handle like that."

He tugged off his glasses and wiped the lenses with a cloth he pulled out of his front pocket. "He wasn't all he appeared to be."

Interesting choice of words. If he wasn't what he appeared, what was he like in private? Surely he had enemies. "It had to be hard working with someone like that."

"It had its challenges." He took a drink of his coffee. I took it as an end to that topic.

I moved on to a new line of questioning. "Has the boutique reopened?"

"I believe by this afternoon. There was some talk about the police needing more time to process the area."

"So I guess the police are leaning towards foul play," I said, nonchalantly.

He stood abruptly. "I wouldn't know. I'm an accountant, not a forensic scientist."

Hey, I wasn't either of those, but it didn't take a genius to figure out if the cops were processing your business and wouldn't let you have access, there was more going on than a simple tumble down the stairs. And not to be picky, but I think he meant he wasn't a forensic *investigator.*

I stood and grabbed my cup of chai. "You were probably one of the closest people, other than Quinn, to Mason. You might know if someone wanted to hurt him."

Evan's eye twitched nervously. "If I think of someone, I'll be sure to let the police know."

He sure didn't look like a guy who was willing to answer police questions about his deceased client. Perhaps I was reading too much into all his ticks and twitches and he was just a Nervous Nelly by nature.

"Thank you again for the donation," I said. "We appreciate it. If you decide you want to attend, give me a call."

He gave a half smile. "You really do seem to be a nice person, although you ask a lot of questions. Maybe you and Quinn just got off on the wrong foot."

I shrugged. "Maybe. I was thinking about dropping off a card and flowers. Do you think she'd appreciate the gesture?"

Okay, I hadn't thought about any such thing until he kept saying Quinn didn't like me. The idea of seeing her wasn't about antagonizing her, but I wasn't above annoying her. I wanted to know more about Mason's death, especially if it wasn't an accident. I know, I was supposed to stay out of it. But with Grey's involvement due to MacAvoy's awful "news" report, I was finding it difficult to keep my nose clean.

He pushed his lips together. "Hard to say." He leaned closer unexpectedly and whispered, "Just between you and me, they weren't getting along lately. The card might be too sympathetic. Anytime Mason wanted to get back on her good side, he'd bring her a bouquet of roses. White."

"I appreciate the advice."

As grateful as I was to be off the hook for a card full of false sympathetic words, I wasn't romancing her, so white roses were off the table. A nice arrangement of wild flowers should get me an audience with Quinn. I was curious about her and Mason's relationship.

As the old saying goes, when there's foul play afoot, the spouse is always the prime suspect.

CHAPTER SEVEN

After a quick stop at the drug store to pick up a box of Latex gloves, another Betty request, I stopped by Darby's studio to tell her I'd hired Colin. I was grateful for her recommendation, but even more thankful that Darby had a decent man in her life. The studio was closed, so I sent her a quick text filling her in and asking if she wanted to meet up for lunch. Before I got caught up in the activities of the day, I shot a text to Ella with Angels with Paws letting her know I had Mason's donation, and I would drop the check off later that day.

I arrived at the boutique shortly after eleven to find Betty had opened on time and we already had a handful of customers. Grey was nowhere to be seen.

After making sure our customers had everything they needed, especially the couple with the handsome Australian Shepherd, I went to the office to tuck the donation check safely away until I was ready to deliver it. I pushed open the office door and caught my breath.

I took a couple of steps inside then stopped, taking in the view. Betty had taken it upon herself to rearrange my desk. My seemingly disorderly piles of invoices, special orders, and merchandise ideas had disappeared. My usual messy desk was now clutter free. How in the world was I going to find anything? I turned around only to find Betty blocking the doorway. She reached for the box of gloves I held.

I yanked my hand back. "Why?" It was the only word that came to mind.

Her sunset-orange-colored eyebrows, which significantly clashed with her periwinkle loungewear, lifted questioningly. "Did you want to clean up the mess Jax left by the plush throw toys? It's a doozy."

Jax must have been the Australian Shepherd. I pointed to my desk. "Why did you do this?"

She wrinkled her nose. "Why are you so cross, Cookie?"

"I'm not cross. I'm annoyed."

"Oh, there's a difference?" she mumbled loud enough for me to hear. "You can fill me on how those are nothing alike later. Gimme the gloves."

"How am I going to find anything? You've moved my papers, invoices, notes, and stashed them who knows where —"

Betty slipped past me with a shake of her head. "I shoved them in that top drawer over there. My new partner in crime stopped by earlier and said he needed a place to take care of his gallery work. He called it a 'hot desk.' " She snorted. "A hot desk for a hot guy. If you know what I mean."

I wasn't finding her amusing at the moment. Hot desk? There was no way I was rotating my desk space with anyone. Not even Grey. He was not going to come in here and take over my office.

"There's no need to give him that much space. You cleaned off my entire desk. He's only going to be here for a couple of weeks. How much room does one laptop take up?"

"My new partner needs a place to work. And you weren't in a hurry to give him that."

"That's not true," I lied automatically.

"You're hidin' something, and so is that handsome man of yours. I'm sure you've got your reasons for keeping your secrets, but don't lie to me." A tinge of hurt hid behind her confused tone.

I sighed. The last thing I wanted was to hurt her feelings. "It was very thoughtful of you to help Grey, and you're right. I'm not in a hurry to let him into my private space. But it's not a secret why."

"Sure, sure," she said.

I could feel her watching me intently as I pulled out a stack of paperwork she'd shoved into the drawer. Grey had his work cut out for him keeping Betty in the dark about his secret life.

"You ever gonna forgive him for breaking your heart?"

"Already forgiven. It's just time to move on, and it's hard to do that with him hanging around." I exhaled, releasing my frustration. It wasn't Betty's fault Grey was ramrodding his way back into my life and I was confused about how I felt about it. "You should go take care of our customers."

"Uh-huh." She didn't sound convinced. "While I have your attention," she began, "are you ready to talk about your grandmother's ugly brooch? I hid it away in my bank safety deposit box. You just let me know when you've changed your mind and aren't going to give it to that sassy cousin of yours, and I'll take you to it."

I sized her up. "That's what you said last month. It's my brooch. I don't need to prove anything." I handed her the box of gloves and motioned for her to leave. "Let's go take care of our customers."

"Lookie here, Cookie. I didn't convince that crazy Mrs. Swanson into handing the brooch to me, just to have you turn it over to Carol," she said over her shoulder as we made our way to the front of the store. "If I wanted her to have it, I'd have let her deal with those two on her own."

I ignored that she had purposely gotten Caro's name wrong. It was just Betty's way. But it was her fault the Swansons had the heirloom in the first place. Had she not lost it while we were glamping, it would be safely hidden away somewhere at my house. Only she had lost it, and Mr. Swanson had found it. The old coot had a gambling problem, and once he'd learned the true value of the brooch, instead of returning it to the rightful owner — me — the rat had tried to auction it off to Caro and me. No way either of us was about to buy something that belonged to us in the first place.

When we didn't fall for his scheme, Betty had gone behind our backs, paid Mrs. Swanson a visit when her husband was out, and convinced her to hand the brooch to Betty.

I lowered my voice. "No one asked you to poke your nose into our feud."

Somehow Betty had it in her head that

she was the one to decide the rightful owner of my grandmother's brooch. Caro and I had spent more years than I cared to count fighting, arguing, and stealing the antique pin from each other. Now Betty held it hostage.

She scoffed. "Someone needed to save you from yourself."

What?

"I found the gloves," she announced to Jax and his human parents. Betty pulled a glove out of the box she carried and tugged it over her hand. With a loud snap of the glove, she announced she was ready.

"We're so sorry," the short brunette apologized unnecessarily. "Jax is normally better behaved. My husband already took care of it." She held up a roll of doggie waste bags.

"Don't worry about it," I said. "It happens more than you'd think. If you need anything, don't be afraid to ask."

Jax and his parents blissfully rummaged through the larger dog toys.

The gentleman looked up and smiled. "You have a nice selection."

"We just got in a new shipment of treat jars." Betty pointed to the display with her gloved hand. "Hottest item in town."

His lips twitched. "We'll be sure to check

them out."

"You might want to take off the glove," I said to Betty.

"I think I'll clean off the counter first. I'm gloved and ready to clean." She made her way behind the counter. She grabbed the glass cleaner and rag and started to wipe down the glass top in a tiny circular motion.

I followed her. "What did you mean by someone needed to save me?"

"You were gonna throw in the towel. Why would you stop fighting for your inheritance?"

"Where did you get that crazy idea?"

She stopped her baby circles. "You said you were going to give your pin to Carol."

"I never said that. I was thinking about it. Grey believes it's the right thing to do. That I should offer it to *Caro* as a peace offering."

She waved the wet rag in front of her in irritation. "What does he know? He's good looking, but he doesn't know the first thing about family drama."

I nodded. "Then it's settled. You'll bring the brooch to the shop tomorrow."

Betty studied me, head tilted, eyebrows raised. She shook her head. "I don't think so. I think I'll keep it until you tell me what secret you and Grey are hiding."

It felt like a rock had settled in my stomach. The havoc she could create if Loose Lips Betty ever found out about Grey's undercover work was limitless. "I told you there is no secret."

"You're lying like a con man. Tick tock, tick tock." She clucked her tongue.

"What the heck does that mean?"

"Time's running out, Cookie. Time is running out."

The only time I was running out of was time for lunch.

The afternoon whizzed by. True to his word, Colin sent several photos of him and Missy chilling on the couch and a short video of their play time at the beach. Any reservations I'd had about hiring him dissolved as I watched the twenty-second video for the hundredth time.

It was well after three o'clock when Betty, tired of my stomach growling, kicked me out of the shop to grab a bite to eat.

I stopped by Darby's studio to see if she'd like to join me. Luckily, she was in and had skipped lunch that afternoon to drop Fluffy off at the trainers. Fluffy had landed the Disney role. She was off at rehearsal and a wardrobe fitting.

Once Darby had locked up, we walked up the street to our favorite deli. She looked especially fashionable today in her distressed jeans with embroidered flowers, white t-shirt, and brown, felted hat. I wore my favorite pair of boyfriend jeans, flats, and a t-shirt that read "The Dogmother." Once we reached the sandwich shop, we ordered our food and looked for a free table. I was surprised at the number of people eating so late in the day.

We found a small round table outside on the hedged patio that faced PCH, and sat across from each other. The bright sun blared through the trees directly onto the eating area. We both slipped on our sunglasses. My stomach growled as I dug in to my tuna sandwich.

Under the small brim of her felted hat, Darby's face glowed. It could have been the cheerfulness of the sun, but I believed it had more to do with the new man in her life.

"I knew Missy and Colin would hit it off," she gushed. "He really likes her. He said she had a spunky personality."

"Are you sure he was talking about my dog?" I joked.

She laughed easily. "Don't worry, he liked you, too. Isn't he great with animals?"

Darby chatted on about how they texted throughout the day and that he had filled her in on taking Missy and me on as new clients, never touching her ham and Swiss sandwich.

While she continued to carry the conversation, I polished off my tuna sandwich, kosher dill pickle, and a small bag of salt and vinegar chips. I pushed my plate to the side of the table and smiled while she excitedly talked about how Colin had managed to coax Fluffy into eating her gourmet lunch from a dog bowl.

"Now, that's impressive." I wasn't being sarcastic. It was impressive. Fluffy normally ate from a Waterford crystal bowl. The Afghan hound acted like she was above all dog-type activities. It wasn't all her fault. Her original owner had treated Fluffy as if she were her child, not a beloved pet.

I pointed at Darby's plate. "Do you want me to ask for a to-go box?"

She glanced at her barely touched lunch. "Oh. I should stop rattling on about my life and eat."

I smiled. "You're happy. That's not a crime. You were right. He has a strong connection to animals. I appreciated how he interacted with Missy, letting her come to him on her terms. He has a great deal of patience." But there was still something about him that had me unsettled.

I waited until she'd swallowed the bite she'd taken before I asked, "How serious are you two?"

Darby picked at the multigrain crust. "He asked me out for breakfast tomorrow morning."

I blinked, not expecting that answer. "Oh?"

Darby blushed. "No. No. We are nowhere near that type of relationship. We both have late appointments the next few days. He's obviously busy in the afternoons, so . . . ah, he suggested a breakfast date."

"Everyone loves eggs and bacon. You can learn a lot about someone by what they eat for breakfast."

"You think so?"

"Absolutely. A breakfast burrito means he's a multitasker, avocado toast means he's too trendy for us. Sugar cereal, still a kid at heart and may have commitment issues. Omelet with dry wheat toast, he's got health issues he doesn't want you to know about. Bacon, egg, and cheese sandwich, he knows what he likes and isn't afraid for you to know."

Amused by my breakfast personality quiz, she asked lightheartedly, "What does Grey have for breakfast?"

I rolled my eyes. "Greek yogurt, scrambled eggs, and a bowl of fresh fruit. He's health conscious and extremely disciplined."

She cocked her head to the side. "Your breakfast of choice is eggs, bacon, and pancakes. Let me guess, that means you're the all-American girl next door."

I laughed. "I'll take that. And your favorite breakfast is oatmeal with fresh organic blueberries — you're an old-fashioned girl with a giving heart."

She wrinkled her nose. "I guess that's a compliment."

"Of course it is."

I relaxed under the warmth of the sun, glad Darby was taking her time finishing her lunch.

"Did I tell you I met with Ella Johns about the film festival next month? She asked if I'd be the official photographer," Darby said between bites of her sandwich.

"That's great. Please tell me you said yes."

She nodded. "Red carpet events can be a little stressful, but they are fun. Did you hear they're trying to get A-list starts Sal Poochino and Dina Sweetin to attend as special guests?" She bit into her dill pickle with a loud crunch.

"Ella had mentioned it. I'd read that Dina

Sweetin is a big advocate for pet adoption. Ella's mother, Anastasia, and Dina were good friends back in the day. Knowing that, it could happen."

Anastasia Johns was the founder of Angels with Paws. She had worked in the costume and wardrobe department on the film, *The Godfather,* which is where she'd met the famous actors. Like a large segment of Laguna residents, Anastasia was an avid animal rescue activist.

When her daughter, Ella, started to have seizures at the age of ten, Anastasia had purchased a seizure alert dog, Checkers, who helped Ella regain her confidence and live a normal childhood. Anastasia was determined every child who wanted a Checkers of their own should have one. That's when she founded Angels with Paws to help families that couldn't afford a response dog. After Anastasia passed away, Ella took over and started awarding college scholarships.

"Do we tell Betty?"

Betty had been very vocal about inviting celebrities to the main event. "We'll have to at some point. Speaking of Betty, do you have any idea what she's been up to?"

Darby shook her head. "I'm afraid to ask, but too curious not to. What's going on?"

"Normal Betty shenanigans. She disappears for a minimum of an hour almost every day, doesn't tell me where she's going or what she's doing. You remember the last time that happened?"

"Raider."

"Exactly. She rescued a Saint Bernard larger than she is. There's no telling what she could be hiding."

Darby leaned back in her chair and crossed her legs. "Maybe she'll tell Grey what she's up to while you're gone."

"Maybe." I started thinking about our possible special guests next month. "If Ella manages to book a couple of Hollywood stars, that no-good MacAvoy will do his best to get an exclusive interview."

"That's not necessarily a bad thing," Darby hedged, always willing to play the role of Pollyanna. "News coverage is good publicity. Free publicity."

My eyes widened, surprised she would defend Mr. TV. "There's no guarantee he'll provide positive coverage. I don't trust him to represent the event in a favorable light. He's always looking for an unflattering angle to drum up unnecessary drama. Case in point, last night's segment where he insinuated Grey is involved in Mason's death."

Darby placed her empty plate on top of

mine. "You saw that, huh?"

"It was awful. He better not show his face at the boutique any time soon."

"Do you think Grey has seen it?"

I shrugged. "Probably. That's his default TV station. It would be hard not to."

"Have you heard from him?"

I shook my head, releasing a heavy sigh. "He was at the shop earlier today while I was out. Betty rearranged my desk to make room for him."

Darby made a face. "I take it you didn't handle either very well."

"Not at all. Let's talk about something less entertaining than my earlier overreaction. I got the check from Quinn and Mason's bookkeeper, Evan. Seems like a decent enough guy."

"Now, that is great news."

"I thought I'd stop by Hot Handbags once it's reopened this afternoon to thank Quinn for the donation and to pay my respects."

Darby pulled her sunglasses down and eyed me. "I believed you until you said, 'pay your respects'."

I tilted my head and asked, "Was it my delivery? I can work on that."

"It was the word 'respect'," she deadpanned. "What are you up to? Does this have something to do with Grey?"

Whoa. She sounded like Betty with all the questions. I was starting to sweat, and it wasn't because of the heat. I took a drink of my water. "I thought that while I'm there, I might just ask a few questions about Mason's death."

She tapped her fingers on the Formica table. "I'd tell you to stay out of it, but I know it would fall on deaf ears, so I'm going to tell you to make sure Grey and Malone don't find out."

I held up crossed fingers. "Wish me luck. Or you could join me? Be my lookout."

She readjusted her shades. "As much fun as that sounds, I'll have to pass."

"That leaves me with Betty as my last option for a backup."

"I don't see you doing that to yourself."

I laughed. "True. So, what's more exciting than ruffling Quinn's feathers?"

"Nina Fernandez loves the costume you sold her for Dash so much she booked a photo session of the two of them in their Dogfather outfits. She plans to use one of those photos for her Christmas card this year."

"Oh, what a lovely idea. I want to do something like that, too, for the shop's customers. Would you take some candid photos of Betty and Raider, and Missy and me at the boutique when I get back from Dallas?"

Darby smiled excitedly. "Yes!"

We pulled out our phones and checked our calendars. We agreed on a couple of dates. I promised to talk with Betty to see if either of the days worked for her. We cleared off our table, and after a quick hug good-bye, we parted ways. I hopped in the Jeep and raced toward the flower shop, brimming with the spirit of adventure.

CHAPTER EIGHT

I roamed Violet's Buds 'n Blossoms, undecided on what to buy. Although the florist shop was on the smaller side, they had an expansive variety, which was why they had been voted number-one local florist for three years running.

As much as I appreciated Evan's suggestion to reach out to Quinn, his recommendation of white roses was never a possibility. I'd changed my mind about my original idea of wild flowers. Now, I vacillated between an arrangement of lilies and another of orchids. I settled on a completely different choice — a potted Easter lily plant. Obvious, but in this situation I was okay with it.

As I drove to Hot Handbags with my sympathy offering safely seat-belted in the passenger seat next to me, I thought about how Quinn had managed to lie low and stay out of the news since Mason's death. I couldn't recall a single interview or photo of her in the paper or on television. At first blush, hiding from the press seemed like a good idea. But if Mason had been murdered, wouldn't she make at least one public plea for information leading to an arrest?

I reached the shop but had to circle the block a couple of times before I snagged a parking spot. I slipped inside the busy store unnoticed. Hard to believe since I was carrying a three-foot plant. I took in the activity and quickly concluded most people weren't there to purchase designer accessories, but to shop for gossip. Lordy, could I relate. I recognized a number of Bow Wow customers who were known to seek scuttlebutt on the latest scandal rather than buy high-end pet products. Possessing my own nosey nature, I didn't hold it against them.

I spotted Quinn near a display of Dolce & Gabbana square bags that most women would consider luxurious arm candy. (I counted myself in that group.) I expected her to have red-rimmed eyes and exhibiting distraught behavior . . . the bereaved widow act played to the hilt. But that wasn't the case.

Instead, Quinn was holding court in her skinny white jeans, white linen blouse, and gold flats. A reasonable choice of footwear after her almost fall down the stairs and her husband's undetermined cause of death. That she was wearing white and not traditional mourning black wasn't lost on me. Not that she had to wear black. I watched her for a few minutes as she charmed her customers and ordered her staff around. For the first time since I'd known her, she had an authentic smile that reached her eyes. Thinking badly about the wife of a dead guy was easy when she doesn't look devastated or suffering over the loss of her husband, but instead looked . . . energized.

I shifted the Easter lily plant from one arm to the other and pushed past a small group of women huddled around the beach totes. Their whispered concerns about my presence at the shop trailed behind me. I didn't recognize them as Bow Wow customers, but from their hushed tones, I could tell they knew me. Or should I say knew about my relationship with Grey? Damn MacAvoy.

My gaze followed Quinn as she flittered from a couple of L.A.-type fashionistas worshiping at the Coach bags to a short, mug-faced man with gray slicked-back hair and dark slashes for eyebrows. Judging by Quinn's suddenly stiff shoulders and hardened face, he wasn't someone she wanted to see. Interesting.

Mid-conversation, Quinn caught my eye and immediately stopped talking, her lips set in an irritated line. The man turned to see what had distracted her, and slowly smiled in my direction as I approached them. His polished flamboyance in his all-black outfit shouted mobster or bad actor. We were close to L.A, so I settled on actor.

"Mel, congratulations on the new side job," she drawled. "Deliveries suit you."

Everyone wants to be a comedian. I viewed my new knowledge that she didn't like me as a challenge. I smiled brightly. "I wasn't sure if there'd be a service or not. I hope you like lilies."

I shoved the potted plant in her direction, which Quinn reluctantly accepted. I held back a satisfied grin as a soft bloom annoyingly rubbed her cheek.

She brushed the offending lily away. "A plant. How . . . practical."

Practical had never been a personality trait used to describe me. Ever.

An uncomfortable silence settled between us. I guess that was the extent of the thank-you she'd extend in my direction. I tried to keep in mind she had just lost her husband, but I didn't think that loss had affected her current attitude toward me.

"I'm glad you like it. My Texas mama

hammered into me that grieving widows always appreciate gifts that remind them of their loved one. A plant does that much better than flowers or roses, don't you think? Those can be so . . . pretentious."

The short man snickered. Quinn ignored him. She narrowed her eyes, pinning me with warranted irritation. "Why are you here? Evan said he already met with you. Didn't you get what you wanted?"

Wow, tough crowd. I swallowed a sarcastic comment climbing its way out of my mouth. "I did. Along with expressing my condolences" — I pointed at the plant — "I wanted to personally thank you on behalf of Angels with Paws for the sponsor —"

"I'll go put this upstairs with the others," she interrupted. With a sharp turn and a loud putout sigh, she trudged toward the back of the store effectively rebuffing me.

"Was it something I said?"

The strange man held out his hand. "I don't believe we've had the pleasure, Mel."

He smelled like . . . egg rolls? My intuition said he wasn't someone I should be on friendly terms with. And it wasn't because he smelled like Chinese takeout. I always trusted my gut. "Melinda," I corrected.

He let loose a deep chuckle. "My apologies for assuming familiarity. Leo Montana,

144

import-export. It's clear you're not a friend of Quinn's. You must have been a friend of Mason."

I was curious what he meant by import-export. After dating Grey for so many years, I'd learned there was a wide range of import services, from travel to computer, and export products, from car parts to wine. The way Leo Montana had slipped in that piece of information so easily, it made me think he had his own agenda and — forgive the expression — was priming the pump.

"We weren't exactly friendly." I waited for him to offer an explanation of his relationship with Quinn, but he didn't. So I asked, "What about you? Are you a friend of Quinn or Mason?"

"Both. A long-time family friend."

This would have been when he twirled his moustache or adjusted his lapel carnation if he'd had one.

"Really? They've only been here for about a year. You must have known them when they lived in . . . I just realized I didn't know where they're from."

He shrugged square shoulders. "Here and there. Judging by Quinn's treatment, you're either a business rival or you had a thing for her dead husband."

I recognized a non-answer when I heard

one. And then he deflected with a goading question disguised as a statement. Obviously, we were both seeking information. What was he hiding? And was it about him or Quinn?

I remained on guard. "Neither. I own Bow Wow Boutique down the street."

"Ah, yes. Bugsy, my dog, and I have walked by there a number of times. We'll have to pop in. You can say hello to my little friend."

I couldn't help myself; I laughed. "That's a great name. What kind of dog?"

"Oh, a little of this, a little of that. A street-smart rescue." His eyes twinkled as he talked about his pup.

I understood the emotion behind the words. Friend or enemy, we all loved our four-legged best friends. "Those are the best kind."

Maybe I was judging him too harshly. I immediately squelched that line of thinking. I narrowed my eyes. He had quickly assessed how to get me to drop my guard. He was clever.

"Don't know where I'd be without him," he continued. "He's getting his weekly massage right now. Maybe we'll stop by later today. You can show me your top sellers.

I'm always interested in what's selling these days."

Was he looking for something new to export? Perhaps he was also an investor of some type. Whatever his interest in our best sellers, I'd have to keep him away from Betty, knowing her recent penchant for purchasing a large quantity of new merchandise. And she'd also find him strangely attractive.

"Trust me, I'll keep an eye out for both of you," I promised.

He looked around the shop. "Looks like Quinn ditched us."

"Or she got sidetracked with a customer," I countered.

"Hmm. Possibly. Tell me, do you think she has a steady flow of traffic?"

I shrugged as I looked around the busy store. People weren't truly shopping, but mingling around the merchandise holding intense gossip sessions. "I suppose." You can have great traffic, but if you don't have buyers it doesn't matter how many people walk through the front door. "What does Quinn say?"

He ignored my question, asking one of his own. "You look like someone who knows a good handbag. What do you think of her merchandise?"

I eyed him suspiciously, uncertain how to take the statement about me recognizing a "good" handbag. The whole line of questioning was curious, but I played along willing to see what he had up his sleeve.

"From what I've seen, she has a decent high-end selection of purses that appeal to tourists and locals. It appears she's turning over items at a steady clip as there's frequently new inventory. But again, I'm not around very often. What I think is new inventory could simply be rotating stock so it looks like she has new inventory."

He nodded. "You're smart. What else can you tell me?"

He definitely had an angle, but for the life of me, I couldn't put my finger on it. Suddenly it dawned on me that he could be interested in opening a competing business. "Why are you so interested in Quinn's store?"

Quinn appeared out of nowhere, with freshly applied lip gloss, so I'd never know if he would have actually answered my question or continued to deflect with his own.

"Leo, I thought you had a meeting to get to. I'm sure Mel doesn't want to hear you blabber on. Your stories are tiresome."

I had a feeling his stories, fiction or true, were anything but boring.

"Forgive me if I've kept you from something with my questions," he said to me. "I do have an appointment in Newport." He adjusted his black suit jacket. "Don't forget about our talk, Quinny. After speaking with the lovely *Melinda,* consider my offer formal."

Quinny? That's rather familiar. It sounded like a nickname a father gave his daughter. I studied Leo closer. He was significantly older than she, but I couldn't make out any family resemblance.

Quinn crossed her arms. "I told you I wasn't interested."

"You were last week," he countered.

She lifted her chin in defiance. "I changed my mind."

"I'm sure I can change it back."

"Don't bother. You'd be wasting your time."

Undeterred by her anger, he tugged her left hand free and blithely kissed the backside, slightly above her wedding ring. "I'll return tomorrow."

She yanked her hand back, clenching it into a tight fist. Leo responded with a deep chuckle. "So spirited. I'm sure that's what Mason found so appealing."

"I won't change my mind." Her voice was as pinched as her nose.

His dark eyes sparkled knowingly. "Ah, but you already have, and we both know it. Ciao."

And with that he waltzed away.

Definitely not her father. What offer was he referring to? Was she or wasn't she going to change her mind? And change her mind about what? Could he have had something to do with Mason's death? It was all over my head, but I was dying to figure it out.

"Quinny" vigorously rubbed off his kiss. Her face flamed as she eyed me. "What did you say to him?"

I shook my head, confused. Was she was angry or embarrassed? "He asked what I thought about your merchandise selection. I said you had a nice variety."

"And . . . what else? You must have said something else." Anger cracked her frosty shell, revealing vulnerability, or was that fear?

"Nothing. I swear. Who the heck is Leo Montana?"

"No one."

The flatness in her voice wasn't fooling me. I pointed to her hands. "You're certainly not acting like he's no one. And if you really want me to believe that, you two need to get your stories straight."

"What does that mean?"

"You're acting like he's a spurned lover who won't take no for an answer. He claims he is a family friend."

She blinked quickly, transforming back to the ice queen I recognized. "He was Mason's friend. Not mine."

I turned toward the front of the shop where Quinn's nemesis had just sailed out the door, and mine suddenly swept inside. My semi-jovial mood evaporated.

"Damn him," I mumbled.

I turned back toward Quinn just in time to see a cat-like smile pounce on her gloss-slicked lips. Her mood instantly improved at my obvious loathing for the local pseudo celebrity.

"You don't like him." She practically purred, happy to turn her attention to me.

I scowled. "I don't like people who lie or spread half-truths."

"Melinda, imagine finding you here," MacAvoy called out behind me.

I flinched hearing his perfectly enunciating, news-anchor voice even though I knew he was there. The untrustworthy snake slithered toward us as if he didn't have a care in the world. A ripple of excited murmurs swept through the shop. My blood pressure spiked. He stopped within an arm's reach of me.

151

I shoved my hands in my back pockets, an effort to resist the temptation to ring his tanned neck. "File any fake news lately?" The taunt fell out of my mouth instantly.

He flashed a cocky smile at me, unaffected. "You saw my report. All facts, by the way. Stay tuned, there's more."

"Not if I can help it," I promised under my breath. Not exactly sure what I could do about it.

"If you have anything to add, I'm always available."

Along with his handy dandy voice recorder covertly tucked away, I was sure.

He turned his attention toward Quinn. "Mrs. Reed, nice to see you again."

Again? Had she been talking with the media after all?

"Any news on Mason's death?" She thawed into a normal human being right before my eyes.

"Nothing has changed. Unless Melinda knows something. Her ex-fiancé is a person of interest."

My face heated. "That's not true." My forceful denial drew unwanted attention to our trio.

"According to my sources, it is. He was seen arguing with Mason. They had a bad business dealing —"

Quinn, wide-eyed and incredulous, pointed her long finger at me. "Grey Donovan is your ex-fiancé? The owner of ACT Gallery?"

Animated whispers flittered through the store.

I lowered my voice. "Yes. And Mr. Fake News here is playing fast and loose with the truth. I was there when Mason and Grey had their disagreement. Grey was clear that if Mason wanted to return the original painting, he'd accept it and give him a full refund, but it had to be the painting Grey had sold him."

"What does that mean?" she asked.

I shifted my weight from one foot to the other. MacAvoy was probably recording everything being said. I had to choose my words carefully. "The painting Mason tried to return wasn't the one Grey had sold him."

"That's utter nonsense. Of course it was. Your fiancé sold him a forgery. Mason told me himself weeks ago."

"No." I shook my head vigorously. "Grey's an honorable man. He'd never be involved in selling . . . imitation art as an original. By the way, how did Mason even know it was a forgery?"

Quinn's gaze bobbed between MacAvoy

and me. She struggled for something to say. "He had it appraised." Her uncertain tone made her comment sound more like a question than a statement. She was guessing. Mason hadn't told her everything.

"That doesn't make sense," I said. "There's no need. It comes with an appraisal for insurance purposes. Why was he having it appraised a second time?"

"He must not have trusted Donovan," Mr. TV butted in.

I shot him a withering look. "If that were true, he wouldn't have purchased the art in the first place, Mr. Know It All. Quinn, you should talk to Evan. As the bookkeeper he would probably know what was going on. Unless Mason was hiding something from him, too."

I had MacAvoy's attention. And Quinn's.

She bristled. "Too? What are you insinuating?"

"What do you know?" MacAvoy's eyes narrowed.

I ignored him and concentrated on Quinn. "It's obvious by your reaction that you don't know why he asked for a second appraisal. I'd heard you two weren't exactly getting along. Were you having marital problems? Was he planning on leaving you?"

I was jumping to conclusions, but I had to

start somewhere, and I needed to lead MacAvoy down a path that didn't include Grey.

"Who told you that?" she demanded, drawing attention to us. "Your ex-fiancé?"

She didn't deny they weren't getting along. Nor that he was leaving her. Maybe I had unwittingly stumbled onto a real lead. I didn't want to reveal my source was Evan. Armed with this new information I wanted to follow up with him myself. I had new questions.

"No. Grey doesn't gossip. But you should talk to him for yourself. Get the truth first hand" — I flashed angry eyes at Mr. TV — "about the art and what happened between them at my boutique."

MacAvoy jumped in. "I'd like to be a part of that conversation."

"No," Quinn and I said in unison.

I knew whom I was protecting. What or whom was Quinn protecting?

"I'd like to get a conversation with him on the record," MacAvoy said. "I have a number of questions for him."

I shook my head. "Not going to happen. Especially after your last stunt."

"That's unfortunate. I have a witness who can place Donovan here shortly before Mason's death."

My head snapped in his direction. I struggled to catch my breath for a second. "Impossible," I managed to choke out. "I can't believe you'd outright lie. Have you no integrity?"

"Who? Who saw him?" Quinn demanded.

"No one. He's making this up, hoping to get other information. That's how he works."

MacAvoy's arrogant expression turned taunting. "Talk to your personal homicide detective. Maybe you'll believe him."

CHAPTER NINE

No longer annoyed by MacAvoy's inflammatory comment about my "personal homicide detective," I brooded over his insistence that Grey had been seen with Mason the morning of his death. If it was true, which I hated to admit that it probably was, why had Grey lied to Malone? What in the world was he doing at Hot Handbags first thing in the morning? More importantly, if Mac-Avoy knew about it, so did Malone. Could that be what he had been questioning Grey about? I rolled my shoulders a couple of times, working out the kinks in my stiff muscles. It suddenly felt like weeks since Mason's death, not twenty-four hours.

By the time I returned to the boutique it was almost time to close for the day, and I still needed to drop off the donation check to Ella. I entered the shop to find Betty and Grey crouched down, heads together, organizing the merchandise on the bottom

157

shelves. The bell above the door announced my arrival.

Grey looked over his shoulder with a warm smile. "Well, hello. You came back," he said as he stood.

Like a bad habit, my heart skipped a beat seeing his handsome face.

Betty tried to spin around but landed on her bottom. "Where you been, Cookie? I was about to call that sexy detective to look for you." She swatted away the hand Grey offered her.

I dropped my tote bag on the counter next to the register. "After lunch with Darby, I stopped at Hot Handbags to thank Quinn for the donation. Where are all our customers?"

Grey's cheek twitched. "You talked to Quinn?"

"Were you investigating without me?" Betty jumped to her feet. Okay, she didn't exactly jump — more like awkward newborn fawn standing for the first time. She held up her hand. "Don't say anything. Let me get my investigator notebook first."

"Whoa. Hold on there. There was no interrogation. I stopped by to thank Quinn for the donation."

I wanted to talk to Grey without an audience. Betty would not only record what I said in her notebook, but she would insist on paying MacAvoy a visit for follow-up comments. My knee-jerk reaction was to blurt out, "Why didn't you tell me you were at Hot Handbags the morning Mason was murdered, Grey? Why did you lie to Malone?" But for once, I held my tongue. It was pure torture keeping quiet about MacAvoy's tidbit of information. Pure. Torture.

Neither Betty nor Grey immediately commented. I held my breath while they both scrutinized me. Knowing me so well, the story I was selling about only visiting Hot Handbags to thank Quinn was difficult to buy.

Betty brushed off her silk periwinkle-colored loungewear. "You disappoint me, Cookie."

Ouch. A twinge of regret gripped me. Maybe I should just tell them both what happened. Grey continued to study me. I could tell by his extended silence that he knew I'd learned something about Mason's death.

"If you'd like to get home to Missy, we can close up. Betty has been showing me the ropes."

Was I being dismissed from my own business?

I tilted my head. "Are you trying to get

rid of me?"

Betty snuggled up to Grey. "Yeah. We're making plans." She wiggled her sunset-orange eyebrows and was already over whatever hurt feelings she'd had minutes before.

Grey wrapped his arm around her bony shoulders and smiled warmly. "She's giving me pointers on how to win back your heart."

God bless her, but why couldn't she leave well enough alone?

"I thought you were Team Cookie?" I looked at Betty pointedly.

She scoffed, nudging Grey with her elbow. "That's why I'm giving Handsome here a list of dos and don'ts. He's got some work to do."

"You're spilling my secrets?" I could always count on Betty to do the opposite of what I wanted her to do.

"Do you have secrets?" Grey's serious tone surprised me.

"Who doesn't?" My flippant tone fell flat.

"Either I'm having a hot flash or the sexual tension between you two is heating up the store. Why don't I close up, and you two get a room?" Betty fanned herself as she walked toward the register.

Betty was right, there was tension between Grey and me, but it wasn't sexual.

I cleared my throat. "Both of you go home, and I'll close up. It's my store. Thanks for holding down the fort while I had lunch with Darby. I appreciate it."

"Well, I'm not going to fight either of you to stay. I'm outta here. Sorry, Handsome, I've got a better offer at home. I've got to let my big boy outside to relieve himself. Raider doesn't like being alone for long periods of time."

While Betty disappeared to the office, I started to cash out the register. Grey finished sorting the plush dog toys.

Betty returned with her handbag. She dropped the bank deposit bag on the counter as she sped past.

"I'll see you both tomorrow. Lock up behind me." And with that she was out the door, no looking back.

"If you'd like to get home to Missy, I'll finish here."

I suspected his offer had more to do with his undercover surveillance — which, by the way, I was now calling *Operation Bow Wow* — than it did about being considerate. I wasn't purposely throwing a wrench into his stakeout, but how could I leave for Dallas if he was a murder suspect? I needed answers.

I turned around and faced Grey. "Why

161

were you at the Reeds' shop the morning Mason was murdered?" I tried to keep my tone from being accusatory.

He tossed the last squeaky squirrel toy in the basket. "Murder? Is that the official word?"

I waited until he faced me. "So, you're not denying it? You were at the shop."

"Are you sticking your nose in Malone's investigation?"

"Hello? Have we just met? Of course. Don't act so shocked. You're avoiding my question, which tells me you were there. Why?"

"We had unfinished business."

"Good grief. Don't talk like that in front of Malone. You sound like a murder suspect."

He looked surprised. "Do you think I had something to do with Mason's death?"

"Of course not. But I'm not the one who can sway public opinion."

"MacAvoy."

My head was starting to ache. I rubbed my temples. "Exactly. He showed up at Hot Handbags, stirring up trouble. I'd like to place a gag order on him."

Grey's eyes crinkled at the corner. "You better hope nothing ever happens to your favorite reporter, or you'll be at the top of

162

that suspect list."

"Well, I'm pretty sure it'll be a long list." I narrowed my eyes. "Don't distract me from the topic. Is this what Malone came to talk to you about? He knew you were the last one to see Mason alive? Besides the person who shoved him down the stairs. And you *lied* to him?"

"I never said I saw him." He headed to the front door and locked it.

"Arg! You make me crazy. Stop with the verbal sparring and just answer the question. Please."

He sighed. "Yes, I went to see him. The door was locked. I knocked. When no one came to the door, I left. End of story."

"So you lied to Malone when he asked where you were that morning?"

"The only way you'd know about that was if you were eavesdropping on our conversation behind a closed door."

"Well I was. And now Malone knows you lied because someone saw you and told MacAvoy. He's planning on running a story about it. He also told Quinn, and let's just say, she didn't take it well."

"He didn't tell you who the eyewitness was?"

"Not a hint. He's a moron. He didn't even consider that the person who saw you could be the real killer and was lying. For some reason he wants to believe the worst about you."

"You said Quinn didn't take it well. What did she say?"

"She was confused. I don't think she knows anything about her husband's little switcheroo with the art. She refused to believe he was capable of purposely trying to pull one over on you. I told her to talk to you about it. I didn't want to say much about Mason's explosion in front of Mac-Avoy."

His blue eyes crinkled at the corners. "Good call."

I smiled. "Thank you. In all seriousness, we have to figure out how to get you off the suspect list. I can't leave for Dallas until I know you're cleared. There's no telling what type of murder investigative fiasco Betty would whip up in my absence."

"You're not going to miss seeing your new niece," he promised, his expression serious.

My head and my heart wanted to believe him. That was a dangerous combination.

His eyes shifted away from my face. "Are you going back there?"

"To Hot Handbags? I wasn't planning on it. Why?"

"Just curious."

Even looking at his profile, I could see the wheels turning in his head. He was planning.

"What are you going to do?"

"Go home to Missy. I'll finish up here."

"You're not fooling me. You want me out of here so you can use my shop to run your covert operation."

"That was the agreement. Now get out of here. The sooner I close my case, the sooner I'll be out of your hair."

That was good news. Wasn't it?

CHAPTER TEN

I woke up the next morning to wet, sloppy kisses.

Missy shoved her cold nose in my face and snorted, demanding I take her outside.

"I'm up. I'm up." I dragged myself out of bed, yanked on my sweats, and pulled my hair into a messy ponytail. I caught a glimpse of my reflection in the mirror and winced. I looked like a complete train wreck. I'd slept hard, exhausted from worrying about Grey and his connection to Mason, and I looked like it.

I rolled my head side to side working out the kinks. "Just once, couldn't you sleep past six?"

Missy wagged her tail and spun in a circle. Woof. Woof.

Her bright round eyes watched me expectantly as if to say, "When a girl has to go, a girl has to go."

I slogged to the bathroom to wash and

moisturize my face. I'd brush my teeth later.

"All right, Girlfriend. Let's go for a walk."

I clipped the lead onto her collar with a loud snap, and we stumbled out the front door. Nose to the damp cement, Missy led the way to the perfect location for her to do her business. I tucked my cold hands inside the sleeves of my sweatshirt. It had rained at some point during the night. The crisp early morning air promptly cleared away my brain fog. Now that I was wide awake, I was immersed in theorizing about Mason's death.

Was Grey the only suspect? Everyone knew the spouse was always suspicious until proven otherwise. I automatically added Quinn to my mental potential suspect list. What about the last person to see Mason alive? Amazon Barbie. Definitely shady.

Since I knew next to nothing about Mason, I couldn't think of a single other name. I started to grasp at straws. Maybe the bookkeeper? What motive would Evan have? I needed to talk to him again. And then there was Leo, the family friend. But I was left with the same frustrating question: why would he want Mason dead? I needed more information.

I'd have to tread carefully. The second Malone figured out I was back to my nosey ways, he'd land on my doorstep. As for Betty, she was already jonesing to grill anyone who had a connection to Mason. She clearly needed to be kept in the dark.

After ten minutes of Missy's intense exploration of the identical three blocks we walked daily, we were home. She raced into the kitchen, her wet paws sliding across the hardwood floor and into her water bowl. She lapped up enough water that we'd be back outside in an hour. The joys of owning a dog. I gulped my small glass of pulp-free orange juice while considering a short run on the beach. Instead, I opted for a twenty-minute home yoga workout. I had a feeling I'd need all the Zen I could get today.

After only fifteen minutes, my face pressed in to a spongy yoga mat while turning myself into a human pretzel, including a handful of minutes in the corpse pose, I wasn't finding my inner peace. I gave up searching for a clear head and decided to get ready for the day.

I ate a spinach omelet full of gooey mozzarella cheese, took a quick shower, and then pulled on a fresh pair of crop jeans and screen t-shirt that read, "Crazy dog lady." Barefoot, I meandered to the kitchen to brew a pot of blackberry tea. I still had a couple of hours before I needed to head to

Bow Wow. It was ten o'clock in Dallas. I put on my big-girl shorts and called Mama to confirm Missy and I would arrive in a little over a week. It was a rare occurrence for my mama to be at a loss for words. For a second I worried she'd fainted. My concern was unnecessary. Her silence was short lived. Once she'd regained her words, she instantly launched into a monologue to convince me to fly home on my daddy's jet. Mama wasn't happy unless she was running my life. Heck, even then I'm not sure that would be enough for her.

I ended the call, worn out from standing my ground. I poured a mug of tea and sat down on the couch. I texted Ella Johns making sure she had found the donation check I'd dropped off last night. I'd just hit send when there was a loud rap at the door.

Missy hopped up and let out a couple of loud non-threatening barks before she returned to lie at my feet. I set my phone on the couch and went to see who was at my door before nine a.m. I peered through the peephole. My heart dropped to my bare feet.

Detective Malone.

Either he'd learned about my conversations yesterday with MacAvoy and Quinn and was here to lecture me about butting into his investigation, or he wanted to question me about Mason's death. Or he had learned Grey had lied to him and wanted to question me about Grey. All bad options.

I inhaled deeply, pulled my shoulders back, and opened the door. "Good morning, Detective." I tried for chipper, but sounded strained. I cleared my throat. "Come on in. I just made a fresh pot of tea. Would you like a cup?" Even in the least desirable circumstances, I was raised to be hospitable. Darn my mama.

"No, thanks. I just came from the Koffee Klatch." No dark circles under his eyes, he smelled freshly showered, and he'd had his morning coffee. Maybe this visit wasn't going to be so bad after all.

He eyed my "Crazy dog lady" shirt, then looked back at me. "Nice."

Malone wore dark jeans and a t-shirt, his normal attire. "I see you didn't dress up for me either. Are you here because you're avoiding Betty?"

"I wanted a private conversation." He looked around my cozy living room filled with low furniture pieces and an area rug. "Is this a good time for a few questions?"

I closed the door behind him. "If I said no, would it make a difference?"

"I'd come back."

170

That was the problem. He'd keep coming back until he got what he wanted. Better to get the interrogation over with, like ripping off a generic Band-Aid that had been stuck to my arm for a week.

I blew my bangs out of my face. "You're not here to give me good news, are you?"

"I'm not here to give you any news. Like I said, I have questions." He was rather serious, even for Malone.

I swallowed my unease. Other than me, Malone was the only other person in town who knew Grey was FBI. He had learned the truth because the FBI had taken custody of Grandma Tillie's brooch during a local murder investigation that *Malone* had been conducting. When the case had been solved, Malone had tried to return the pin to Caro. I had used Grey's contacts, unbeknownst to him, to retrieve it. Of course Malone had gone digging and learned about Grey.

My little stunt was the beginning of the unraveling of my relationship with Grey. An ugly story with an unhappy ending.

I motioned for Malone to have a seat on the couch. He stretched his long legs in front of him. Missy, unimpressed with our visitor, waddled to her dog bed and lay down. I perched myself on the wooden coffee table across from Malone, careful not to brush his leg.

The detective possessed an excellent poker face. Even if he was here to give me news, I doubted it would have been happy news. I decided offense was the best defense.

"I have a few questions of my own. Quinn isn't exactly the grieving widow. Did you know she and Mason had been fighting right before his death?"

He listened, unimpressed. "No."

"I don't know the details," I continued, "but I'd suggest questioning Quinn about her relationship with her husband. It wasn't as wonderful as she led us to believe." I kept my tone light and upbeat, a stark contrast from the dark cloud that had settled over Malone's attractive face.

"Are you investigating?"

I crossed my fingers behind my back. "No. Quinn's bookkeeper is the one who told me they were fighting. He just offered it up. I didn't have to ask."

"Why were you talking with . . ."

"Evan," I supplied quickly. His wooden expression made me nervous.

"Evan, in the first place?"

"Betty had talked Mason into sponsoring the Mobster Film Festival next month. With Mason's death, Evan delivered the check."

"I see."

He was a smart guy. I was sure he did see — right through my nervous explanation. I thought I had succeeded in sidetracking Malone to the point he'd forgotten why he'd stopped by, but that wasn't the case.

"Donovan left before I could get his phone number. You mind giving it to me?" he asked.

The question was innocent enough, had it been anyone other than Malone asking. The detective wasn't the type of guy to forget anything or to let someone leave before he was good and ready. He had an agenda.

"I'd be happy to give him a message for you," I offered.

"I'll take his number." It wasn't a request.

I sighed. "I don't want to give it to you."

My straightforward response caught him off guard. He almost smiled. "I don't suppose you do."

I leaned forward, propping my elbows on my knees. "We both know you have connections and could get it yourself without my help."

He remained stubbornly silent.

"Can I ask why you want it?"

He raised his brows.

"Besides the obvious," I said.

"The obvious reason suffices."

For him, maybe. I couldn't come up with

a single argument as to why I shouldn't hand it over. I hoped I wasn't inadvertently contributing to Grey getting deeper into trouble. I warily walked into the kitchen. Malone followed.

I grabbed one of the many notepads from the junk drawer, tore off a piece of paper, and jotted down Grey's number. Reluctantly, I handed it to him.

He frowned as he studied the paper. "Is this his cell or landline?"

An uncomfortable laugh escaped. "Grey doesn't have a landline. Not even at the gallery. Just his cell." Technically, that wasn't the whole truth. He also had a number of burner phones at his disposal. But I didn't have access to those numbers so I believed that covered me on the partial truth.

He held out the paper. "This is the only number he has?"

"No offense, but are you losing your hearing? It's the only number I have for him."

His brows furrowed. "You gave me the right number, correct?"

I was feeling itchy. Something was up. His persistent questions trigged warning bells. "Of course I did. Okay, what's going on? Why do you keep asking me about his phone number?"

He shoved the small piece of paper in his

back pocket. "Thanks."

I stepped in front of him, blocking him from leaving. "No, no, no. You cannot make a big deal about this and then walk off, leaving my imagination to fill in the awful blanks. How much trouble is Grey in?"

Malone must have heard the quiver in my voice. His face softened. Or at least he wasn't as stone faced. "I can't answer that."

"Is he an official suspect? That can't happen. You know what that would mean to his career."

"I'm following the information where it leads." He took a breath and focused his intense dark eyes on me. "How well do you really know Grey Donovan?"

I stared back, equally intense. "I'd trust him with my life. I know he's not responsible for Mason's murder."

"Are you providing him with an alibi?"

I slowly shook my head, a lock of hair falling in my face. "I wish I could, but no. He didn't have anything to do with Mason's death any more than you did."

He nodded. "For your sake, I hope you're right."

I brushed the hair from my eyes, tucking it behind my ear. "Do you have any idea what really happened to Mason? Did he fall or was he pushed?"

"We're still working on that."

"But you're leaning toward pushed. Otherwise, why would you be here?"

His silence unnerved me. "What are you waiting on before you determine it was murder?" I asked.

"Official autopsy. We should hear by tomorrow."

We both already knew Mason had been pushed. I suddenly realized it was possible that by stalling, he was potentially protecting Grey. Giving him time to get off the suspect list. I wanted to give Malone a big ole kiss. Instead I pulled a glass from the cupboard and filled it with filtered water.

"What can you tell me about Bree Young?" he asked.

I handed him the glass. "Who?"

"The woman with Betty when Mason Reed's body was discovered."

"Oh, the tall blond? Betty called her Amazon Barbie."

His lips twitched. "Had you met her previously?

"Never." I committed the name Bree Young to memory, adding her to my mental list of people whom I wanted to talk to. Not that I had any idea how to track her down.

"Have you talked to her?" I asked.

"Yes."

"And?" I prompted.

He handed the untouched glass back to me. "For a minute, I thought you were sticking your nose into my investigation."

I sighed. "We can take this one of two ways. We can play our little game where you tell me to stay out of it, I'll tell you I am, but once you walk out the door, somehow I find myself smack dab in the middle, sifting through a ton of gossip and information, doing everything I can to clear Grey's name." I took a deep breath and plowed on. "Or we can skip the game and acknowledge I'm already involved."

Malone wasn't happy. The clenched jaw was a dead giveaway.

I tried a new tactic. "Look, I've known you long enough to know you're going to follow the information —"

"Facts."

I rolled my eyes. "Right. You're going to follow the *facts* and come to conclusions that seem right at the time. No offense, but sometimes those 'facts' don't lead to the truth. Especially, if the guilty party wants to make the other party a scapegoat. Or worse, a murder suspect."

"The *fact* is, Donovan was seen leaving the scene."

So he knew Grey had lied. "Eyewitness

testimony is the worst type of testimony. Did this person actually talk to Grey or just see someone who looked like him?"

Malone remained silent.

"You might as well tell me. The minute you walk out that door, I'm going to find Grey."

Not that he'd talk. He'd stare at me with the same blank expression Malone wore at the moment. Did all law enforcement learn to make that face during training? Required course: Blank Expression 101.

"She recognized Donovan," he bit out.

She? Well, well, well. I scowled in an effort to hide my enthusiasm at Malone's uncharacteristic slip of the tongue. "We both know that just because he was seen at the scene doesn't prove he had any part of Mason's death. There's no proof Grey and Mason spoke."

"How do you know what proof I have or don't have?"

I twisted my lips. "Point made." I decided to ask for the moon. "Any chance you'll share information?"

"Zero."

It was worth a try. "I know it's not your department, but any word on the break-ins?"

"We're following a couple of leads, but

nothing solid. Have you heard anything new?"

"Other than MacAvoy's claim that the police have a sketch of a possible suspect? No."

"He said that?"

"Made a special trip to the boutique. He couldn't wait to share that little tidbit of info. He's hoping the break-ins are connected with Mason's death."

"Huh."

That was it? He wasn't going to confirm or deny the sketch? "No comment?"

"No. Keep your eyes open and doors locked." He looked concerned. "Betty doesn't still carry a gun, does she?"

"No. Her son-in-law took it back from her after all the craziness at the Dachshund races."

"Good. She's not serious about becoming an investigator, is she?"

"Absolutely." I almost told him about her investigation notebook, but I decided against it. He had enough on his mind.

"Keep her on a tight leash." He turned to leave. I followed him to the door.

"Where are you headed to next?" I asked in a last ditch effort to pry information from him.

He actually chuckled. "Do you ever give up?"

"Never."

"Take care of yourself, Melinda."

I sighed. Can't blame a girl for trying.

CHAPTER ELEVEN

I called Grey to warn him about my unexpected visit from Malone. He didn't answer, and I didn't leave a message. It didn't seem prudent knowing he was currently under the microscope of Laguna Beach's finest.

I said good-bye to Missy, leaving her curled up on her dog bed, knowing Colin would stop by in a few hours to take her for a play date at the Bark Park. I jumped into the sun-warmed Jeep and headed straight for the boutique. Ten minutes later, I pulled up and parked just as a jovial Lenny and his chubby dachshund, Barney, were walking past the shop. Lenny, wearing cargo shorts, t-shirt, and flip-flops, turned and waved. As usual, Barney was in full costume. Today he was a dressed like a white rabbit with fairy wings.

I locked up the Jeep and swept into the boutique. I ditched my shoulder bag under the counter and immediately pitched in to help Betty with the small crowd. We had a good run of customers for a couple of hours. A number of regulars stopped by to pick up special orders, and a handful of tourists poked around checking out our merchandise.

Betty, dressed in a lively Hawaiian-print ensemble with matching icy-pink eyebrows, held up her end of our agreement, pushing the porcelain treat jars to anyone who could fog a mirror. Surprisingly, the jars ended up being a popular item. So much so, Betty suggested we raise the price. I nixed that idea. Instead, I pitched the possibility of throwing in a free dog sweater, but Betty was certain that would slow the "chi" of her sales. I couldn't deny it any longer; the time had come to donate the sweaters to a dog shelter in northern California.

During a late-morning lull, I retreated to my office. Elbow deep in spreadsheets and inventory numbers, I heard Betty's laughter filter down the hallway. It wasn't her normal cackle. This was a flirtatious giggle, like a young girl's mating call. *Uh-oh.* I pushed back from the desk and jumped out of my chair. I quickly made my way to the front of the store, prepared to rescue an innocent man from Betty's zealous clutches.

Instead, I stumbled upon Leo Montana,

who was far from innocent, standing a hair's breadth from Betty. Not one iota bothered by her quirky look and attire. He'd brought his dog, Bugsy. Bugsy wasn't the ragtag mutt I had pictured in my head, but a dapper-looking miniature pincher sporting a red-and-white polka-dot bow tie. The little guy lay contently in the crook of Leo's arm, pointy ears at attention.

"Hello," I greeted, slipping between Leo and Betty, purposely separating them. Although I wasn't sure whom I was protecting from whom. I refrained from the automatic line that it was good to see him. I wasn't one-hundred-percent convinced he might not have a hidden agenda.

I held my hand, palm up to the dog. "This must be Bugsy."

At hearing his name, the smallish Min Pin lifted his head. He sniffed intently. Deciding I passed the sniff test, his tiny pink tongue bathed the palm of my hand. He must have smelled the treats I'd grabbed for Missy.

Leo was dressed in charcoal slacks, dark silk button-up shirt, and tasseled loafers. With his gray hair slicked back, he was only missing a gold chain to complete his throwback-to-the-seventies look. Possibly the reason Betty found him so attractive.

183

"Melinda, you didn't tell me about your lovely business partner." His charismatic tone and scent of egg roll grease filled the shop. What was with the Chinese food?

Business partner? I shouldn't be surprised she'd given herself another promotion. At this rate, by the end of the week, she'd be the sole owner and I'd be the part-time help.

I eyed Betty. She actually blushed under Leo's charming attention. I knew she'd be enamored with him. She loved the bad boys.

"Isn't he hot stuff?" Betty shoved away from me. "Keep your hands off, Cookie."

Seriously? "Not a problem."

Betty snuggled closer to Leo, slipping her arm though his. She rubbed his forearm. "I like your choice of fabric."

Bugsy lifted his head and looked at her. She patted him softly and told him he was a good little dog. I tried to imagine Raider, a rambunctious Saint Bernard, and teeny Bugsy interacting. I cringed. I didn't foresee that to be a successful playdate.

"Leo is coming to the Mobster Film Festival. We're going to meet up. Isn't that right, Big Fella?"

Leo patted her hand tenderly. "The delightful Ms. Foxx has agreed to accompany me."

When did that happen? They'd just met.

This possible relationship was moving too fast.

"What do you think about that, Cookie? I've got a date." My feisty assistant jutted her chin, announcing she'd finally snagged her man.

Their date was in a month. Way too long to listen to her fawn over a potential love interest, yet plenty of time to get her to change her mind if he turned out to be a conman.

"Oh!" She bounced on the toes of her sneakers excitedly. "We should double date with Cookie and her handsome man."

"Grey and I aren't going together," I said, then quickly changed the topic back to Leo. "Is there anything specific you're looking for now that you're here?"

He unlinked his arm from Betty in one smooth motion. "I'm open to suggestions."

"I've got all types of ideas." Betty fluffed her white hair, wagging her lipstick eyebrows at Leo.

He shared a mischievous grin with his true love of a whole five minutes. "I can't wait to hear them."

Well, I could.

"We were talking about dog accessories," I reminded them.

"She's a real party pooper." Betty pouted.

"You need to loosen up, Cookie."

"Cookie? I like that. Fitting." Leo surveyed the boutique with a discerning eye. "I like what you've got going on here, Melinda. A number of local products, top quality, a wide variety of merchandise."

"Thanks. I'm rather proud of it. Feel free to let Bugsy roam around."

His little dog squirmed excitedly as Leo set him down. The Min Pin trotted straight for a basket of dog toys and jumped inside to lie down. He blended in with the toys perfectly. He was adorable. Too bad Darby wasn't here to snap a photo. The image would have made the perfect postcard or calendar picture.

Leo inspected the designer water bowls stacked on the end-cap he faced. His thick fingers gripped the bowls, testing their durability. "Very nice. You've been in this location for a while?" He moved past the collar and leash display, walking toward the pawlish and cologne.

"A few years."

He nodded, digesting my answers. "I'm sure you have a loyal customer base."

I frowned. "Sure."

I grew more annoyed as he continued to analyze my business. It felt like I was in his crosshairs for a hostile takeover. Betty must have picked up on my irritation. She sidled up next to Leo, taking a bottle of pawlish from him and returning it to the shelf.

"Bugsy is a stylish guy, but Yappy Hour Red isn't exactly his color. We have a number of fine-looking bow ties over here. Come with me."

"I'll follow wherever you lead, My Dear."

Was it me or was there a little more swing in Betty's hips as she guided him across the room? The more attention Leo showed Betty, the more she sounded like a young doe-eyed girl.

"Have you considered expanding?" he asked me over his shoulder.

"I'm not really interested."

Betty spun around and grinned. "Think about all the stuff I could buy, Cookie." Her eyes glazed over, mentally spending my money on dog products.

"Trust me, I am," I deadpanned. "Thanks, but we're happy where we are."

He whispered in Betty's ear.

She giggled. "You're my kinda guy, Leo Montana."

He fished a business card from his wallet and walked it over to me. "If you change your mind, I know a guy who owes me a favor. He can find you a deal."

"I'll keep that in mind." I accepted the

card, happy to have his contact information. I might need it in the near future.

The card simply stated, "Leo Montana, Import/Export Expert," and listed his email and phone number. It was the graphic that caught my attention — the world on a string.

"No problem," he said smoothly. "He knows what he has to do if you decide you're interested."

Has to do? He sure had a way with words.

"What's your top seller, My Dear?" he asked Betty.

She tugged him to her new favorite display. "I have the best sales record for pawlish, but this week the top seller is our brand-new porcelain treat jar. A sexy man like you needs one of these. It has multiple uses." She ran her fingers suggestively over the jar.

Oh. My. Gosh. I didn't even want to know where she was headed with that line. I was about to tell her to stop the madness when the bell jingled declaring the arrival of more customers. Thank goodness, I was saved from watching their awkward flirting.

Imagine my surprise when I turned to see Colin and Missy tumble into the store.

"Hey, Girl." I bent down to hug Missy. I snuggled my girl as she excitedly licked my cheek, sandwiched with a few grunts and snorts. Bulldog drool puddled between my feet. She smelled like freshly mowed grass. I assumed they had come from the Bark Park.

"Is everything okay?" I looked up at Colin who stood a few feet away, his hands shoved in his jeans pockets. His light-blue shirt had grass stains on the shoulders.

"Everything is fine."

He didn't look fine. He looked rattled, like his best friend had just died. "I hope you don't mind we drop by for a visit. We finished play time at the dog park. I thought you might like to say hello before we headed home."

If Darby's studio wasn't next door I'd have believed that was the only reason for their stopover. Maybe a talk with Darby would cure what had him so anxious.

"Why don't you leave Missy here while you pop next door and say hello to Darby."

He shifted his weight from one foot to the other. "If you're sure you're okay with that. I'm technically on your time."

Missy broke loose from my snuggling and trotted toward Bugsy. I watched, ready to intervene if needed as the two greeted each other with a curious sniff and nuzzle. Once Missy was satisfied she was still the alpha dog and Bugsy wasn't taking over her territory, she ambled toward the back office, presumably for her bed.

"How about you punch out on the time clock while you're visiting Darby? That only seems fair, don't you think?"

Colin was about to say something when suddenly he caught a glimpse of Leo and Betty at the treat table. His face drained of what little color was left.

Well, I didn't think I was asking too much that I didn't pay for the time he spent romancing my best friend. "Are you okay? You look like you've seen your worst enemy."

"Cookie, my man said he would purchase five treat jars," Betty yelled across the store. Her rosy cheeks reflected her triumph. "I'll get you the ones in the back that haven't been mobbed and breathed on."

She bounced toward the storage room.

Leo joined Colin and me. He looked at Colin quizzically. "You look familiar. Do we know each other?"

Colin swallowed hard. He averted his gaze, suddenly finding the pink diamond-crusted collars interesting. "No, I don't believe we do."

Well, I wasn't a psychic, but judging by Colin's reaction, he did know Leo. I went through the motions, anyway.

"Let me introduce you. Colin Sellers,

meet Leo Montana, import and exports. Leo, this is Colin, Missy's dog sitter. He's new to town."

Leo narrowed his eyes. He shook his head. "I never forget a face."

"I think you have me confused with someone else." Colin's tight voice surprised me. Why would he insist that he didn't know the other man, when it was obvious they'd met before?

"Sellers . . ." Leo was about say something when his eyes widened and he stopped. He quickly composed himself. "Now that you mention it, I think you're right. You do have one of those faces."

Now who was fooling whom? They recognized each other, but neither wanted to admit it. What was going on? I wondered if I should play along or call them out on it.

Colin cleared his throat. "Mel, if you don't mind, I'll be back in a few minutes."

Leo and I watched Colin skitter out of the shop like a scared bunny rabbit.

I didn't mince words. "You know each other."

Leo looked at me with a half-smile. "I thought we did, but I was mistaken."

"No, you're not. Look, he's dating my best friend. If he's hiding something or if he's dangerous, I need to know."

"I'm sure your friend is perfectly safe." He reached out to pat my arm reassuringly.

I stepped back avoiding his patronizing reassurance. He was working too hard to convince me he was telling the truth. I scowled at him. "If he's hiding something, I —"

"We're all hiding something." His joking manner seemed forced.

"No, no we're not." Okay, I was hiding Grey's true job. Betty was being secretive about her personal errand. And of course, Grey. . . . I silently chastised myself for allowing myself to get side tracked. All of that was beside the point.

I narrowed my eyes and pointed at Leo. "If you hurt Betty, I'll hunt you down."

"Is that a threat?" He returned my hard gaze.

"Absolutely."

He let loose a deep laugh, not in the least affected by my threat of harm. "I like you. You've got spunk."

From my peripheral line of vision, I saw Betty come out from the storeroom, struggling with a cardboard box. Her white tennis shoes squeaked across the floor as she staggered toward us.

"Whoa, there," I called out.

Leo and I rushed to her side. I grabbed

the box; Leo grabbed Betty. She patted his clean-shaven cheek affectionately.

"Why didn't you ask for help?" I chastised her. Why did she insist on acting like she was still sixty? I set the box on the counter.

"I told you he wanted five jars," Betty squawked. "Did you think they were going to magically appear? Sheesh."

While I felt like an idiot for not paying closer attention to what she had been up to, Betty made moon eyes at Leo. This flirtation was getting out of hand.

My cell rang, saving me from being subjected to Betty's outrageous ogling. I reached behind the counter and grabbed my phone. "Betty, ring Leo up. I'm sure he has somewhere to be."

She scooted to the register. "We take cash or credit card. Next time you make a purchase, I can give you the friends and family discount."

I rolled my eyes at her offering a discount. "Hello," I answered my cell.

"Hey, it's Grey." The rumble of his deep morning voice made my heart jump.

I wish I had checked the caller ID before I answered. "Hey. You got my —"

"Can you come over?"

I turned my back to Betty and Leo. I tried to decipher Grey's tone, but it was difficult over the phone. "To your house?"

"Yes."

My mind raced with possibilities as to why he'd want me to come over. "Colin stopped by with Missy. Do you mind if I bring her with?"

"I'll see you both in a few minutes." He ended the call without a good-bye.

I shot Colin a text to let him know I had to run an errand and took Missy with me. I didn't want to leave Betty alone with Leo, whom she eyed like a king-sized milk chocolate candy bar. But judging by Grey's tone, I needed to leave now.

"I've got to run an errand," I told Betty. "I'll be back as soon as I can. No funny business while I'm gone."

She glared at me. "Don't forget. I have to leave at one thirty."

"Just like every day for the past three weeks. I got it."

That was another question. Where the heck was she going every day?

194

CHAPTER TWELVE

I couldn't remember the last time Grey had called to invite me to his house. Six, seven months ago, maybe? He lived in the Laguna Beach highlands referred to as "Top of the World," one of the highest points in southern Orange County, where the panoramic ocean view alone could cost a million dollars.

My stomach tightened as I pulled in to the driveway. I shut off the Jeep and looked at Grey's house as if I were seeing it for the first time. Contemporary, custom designed with a European inspiration. Beautiful, inviting, and very Grey. I had the best memories of lounging on the back deck, watching the sun set.

Missy pushed her face against the window and whined. She knew exactly where we were. She pawed at the door, anxious to unload. I unfastened her harness and scratched behind her ears. The second the

Jeep door opened, Missy leapt out, landing in a garden of impatiens and petunias. After a quick shake, she trotted up the stone walk to the front door, eager to get inside.

I grabbed my tote bag and slammed the Jeep door. "You already know the rules," I yelled after her. "Stay off the couch."

I was halfway up the walkway when the front door swung open. Grey stood in the doorway, an image I'd seen a thousand times. Today it was bittersweet. Yesterday's jeans hung low on his hips, his button-down shirt was untucked, his hair mussed, and a large coffee mug in his hand. He looked like he'd just ended a three-day bender. This was not his normal look. Something was up.

Missy raced inside, skirted around Grey, and made a beeline straight to the living room.

"You look like crap." I brushed past him and headed for the kitchen out of habit. I froze mid-step when I realized what I was doing.

Grey closed the door. "It's good to see you too."

We watched as Missy explored tirelessly, ping-ponging from room to room. I knew what she was looking for: the dog bed that used to sit next to Grey's leather recliner.

My heart broke for her.

"Maybe I should have left her at home," I whispered.

"It's in the hall closet."

I looked at him questioningly. "What?"

"Her bed. It's in the closet."

Grey walked down the hallway. Missy stopped searching and froze, head cocked to the side, eyes glued on Grey's movements. Her stocky body trembled when Grey returned with her bed. He set it by his recliner as if it still belonged there. Missy climbed on it, circled a handful of times, tamping down the pillow until it met with her satisfaction. Once she was satisfied, she dropped to her belly with a sigh.

My heart melted. I was such a sucker.

"Thanks for coming," he said, drawing me back to the reason I was here.

I followed him to the kitchen. He offered to make me a chai tea. My heart couldn't take much more of reliving our old routine. He warmed a mug of milk and concentrated chai mixture in the microwave. I refused to question why he still had my go-to mix in his pantry.

"What's happened?"

"I've been removed from the case."

I shook my head. "I must have misunderstood. I thought you just said you were kicked off *Operation Bow Wow.*"

Despite his serious expression, a small laugh escaped. "Operation what?"

I shrugged. "I dubbed your case *Operation Bow Wow.* It seemed appropriate."

He smiled. "I like it." The microwave dinged. He pulled out the mug and handed it to me. "Unfortunately, I'm no longer in charge of *Operation Bow Wow.*"

I leaned against the granite counter. "Why? I don't understand."

"Because I'm a suspect in Mason's death," he said simply. He took a sip of his coffee.

"Malone said you were a suspect?"

"No. But he did give me fair warning I was a person of interest, which got back to the bureau."

"How?"

He shrugged.

I set my tea on the glass-topped kitchen table. "There's no real evidence. What Malone has is circumstantial."

"The paper found in Mason's fist had my cell number written on it."

"So? He bought a painting from you. That's not suspicious."

He ran a hand through his thick hair. "Not my personal cell."

It took me a second before I caught on to what he was saying. I felt sick. Mason had

had a burner number in his hand. That explained all of Malone's questions. I paced the length of the kitchen. Kitchen table to refrigerator, then back again, processing what he was telling me.

"How did he get that number? How did Malone trace it back to you?"

"Malone is a good detective."

"Grey, how did Mason get *that* number? Did you give it to him?"

"Yes."

"Does this have to do with the art piece?" My mind raced for answers. The pieces began to fall into place. "Mason was your undercover operation?"

Grey stayed silent.

I rubbed my face trying to make sense of everything. "Let's start at the beginning."

He sighed. "I'd rather we didn't. Isn't that the t-shirt I gave you for Missy's birthday?" He smiled slowly. " 'Crazy dog lady' still fits you."

I ignored him. "Did Mason really buy that painting from you?"

"Yes."

"Was it really a forgery?"

"What he was returning, yes."

"But if he's dead, and you know he didn't have anything to do with the fake art, why the charade to stay at my shop? The investigation should be over."

"I didn't say the investigation was over. I said I was removed. The new agent will arrive tomorrow. Tom James. He'll be there acting as my overseas art broker for the gallery. Since ACT is still closed for wiring work, he'll need a place to work out of. It should be an easy and believable transition."

I shook my head. "Oh, no. I agreed to work with you, not some stranger."

"Mel, I told you, this was official. Once started, pulling the plug isn't easy."

"But you can't make me agree."

"No."

"Then tell them Mason is dead. So . . . whatever it is you're doing is over, too. Finished."

"But it's not. This case doesn't work that way."

We stared at each other. My chest felt heavy. I pressed my fingers against my temples. I understood what he wasn't saying. "Because your case has nothing to do with the art. The case is about Hot Handbags."

"You know I can't talk about it."

"Why not? You're not involved anymore."

"It's still an active investigation."

"Apparently using my shop. Now run by someone I don't know."

"Agent Tom James. An art broker —"

I held up my hand. "I heard you the first time. Honestly, I don't really care what his name is or what his cover is. I want to know what's going on. Do you trust me or not?"

"You know I do. You also know this has nothing to do with trust."

I resumed pacing. Grey drank his coffee in silence, watching me. In my head I knew he was right. The trust comment was a throw-away argument in order to protect my heart. One thing I'd come to accept over the last few months was that Grey had always trusted me. He had also tried to protect me.

"So Hot Handbags is under investigation. And now Mason is dead. There's a random piece of forged art work in the middle of everything that has nothing to do with the case. Does that about sum it up?"

"Yes."

I sighed. I hated those annoying one-word answers. I drank more tea, thinking about what do to next.

Grey pulled out a chair and motioned for me to sit. "You're making me dizzy with all the pacing."

"Do you think his death has anything to do with the current investigation?" I asked.

He sat in the chair across from me. He

leaned back, stretching out his legs under the table. "I don't know."

"Drugs?"

"What?"

"Are they selling drugs?"

Silence.

"Money laundering?"

More silence.

"Good grief, what's left? Fake handbags?" I laughed at the absurdity of it. Only Grey wasn't laughing with me.

I leaned forward. "No way. Are you kidding me?"

"Come on, Mel." He abruptly stood, turned around, and dumped the remaining coffee in the sink.

"I'm right, aren't I? You're investigating counterfeit purses."

He sighed. "There's a lot of money in it." He turned to face me and crossed his arms.

"That's so brazen. They named their store Hot Handbags. They didn't even try to hide what they were doing. This is right up my alley. Why didn't you ask for my help?"

He raised a questioning brow. "I did."

I nodded. "Fair enough, but not exactly what I meant. I was thinking more about secret shopping."

"I didn't want to get you caught up in it. Besides, we already knew they were selling counterfeit goods. We needed to know where the supply was coming from."

I suddenly remembered the black Chanel clutch in my closet. "I bought a handbag from them. Am I in trouble if it turns out to be counterfeit?"

"No. Which one? Have I seen it?"

I shook my head. "I bought it after we broke up."

"I'd like to see it."

I polished off my tea. If Mason's death was connected with the hot purses, we needed to clear Grey's name. "What exactly does it mean that you're off the case?"

"I can't be near or involved with the investigation."

I tilted my head. "So you can't come to the shop?"

"Technically, I shouldn't." His face was unreadable.

Why didn't I feel relieved Grey wouldn't be invading my space? Wasn't that what I wanted? I felt sad that he wouldn't be able to close the case he started. Worried that he was dependent on Malone to follow evidence without all the facts. And then there was Betty who would be disappointed. She was looking forward to spending time with him. Knowing Grey was going to be at the boutique while I was in Dallas had kept me from worrying about being away and what trouble Betty might get into while I was gone. But that level of reassurance had been pulled out from under me.

"You should know, Malone paid me a home visit this morning."

His shoulders tensed. "What did he want?"

"Your phone number. He also mentioned that it was a woman who saw you that morning at the Reeds' shop."

"Did he give you a name?"

"No. Do you remember seeing a woman hanging around the store? Or waiting in her car for the store to open?"

He thought about it for a few minutes. "No."

I stood and rinsed my mug, then set it in the sink. The longer Grey stayed a murder suspect, the more potential it had to hurt his career. I couldn't believe what I was about to suggest.

"If we really were together, they couldn't keep you away from visiting the boutique."

He looked at me with a big question mark. "Possibly. With our history it would give me a legitimate reason to be there."

I exhaled and jumped in with both feet. "I guess we'll just have to find out."

We stood an arm's length apart, watching

each other. "You're sure about this?" he asked softly.

"Not at all. By the way, I think Betty has a boyfriend."

He whistled softly. "Anyone I know?"

"Ever met Leo Montana? Looks like a character actor from the forties, smells like egg rolls."

He shook his head. "How did they meet?"

"I saw him at Hot Handbags talking with Quinn. Apparently he's a family friend. He asked what I did, and I told him about the boutique. He stopped by with his dog, and suddenly he and Betty are acting like star-crossed lovers. He said he's in the import-export business." Wait a minute! "What about this Leo Montana? A long-time family friend of the Reeds. Import business. When I pressed him for details he gave vague answers. Could he be involved?"

"It's possible."

"But why would he be interested in a dog boutique? Wouldn't that be unorthodox for someone involved in high-dollar crime?"

"I can have someone look in to him."

I shook my head. "I think I'm just being overprotective of Betty. She doesn't always think before she acts."

"We're all protective of her. Let me know if you change your mind."

I sighed. "I think Leo knows Colin, Darby's new boyfriend." I recounted the strange interaction at the shop just a couple of hours earlier.

"It does sound odd. Be careful."

"Since we're 'back together' " — I used air quotes — "can you run a background check on Betty and Darby's new boyfriends?" I batted my eyes.

He shook his head. "I don't think either one of them would appreciate that."

"Darby won't. Betty would be upset she didn't get to run the background check herself."

Grey chuckled. "Talk to Darby about what happened. It's possible there's a perfectly innocent explanation."

"I hope that's the case."

My gut said otherwise.

CHAPTER THIRTEEN

An hour later, I already regretted my proposition to Grey. What had I been thinking? Pretending that we were back together was an insane idea. I'd been against that suggestion since he'd first proposed it. Darn my spontaneous nature. I'd always been the type of gal who takes action. I wasn't into hesitation or watching life passing me by. Planning? I'll be honest, eight times out of then, that was an afterthought.

I decided to focus on the positive. Grey would still be able to babysit Betty. He'd know if this Agent James was doing his job. And best of all, we could concentrate on clearing Grey's name.

Grey asked to keep Missy with him. He wanted the company. He promised to bring her back to my place this evening. I agreed. She couldn't have been in better company unless she was with me. I texted Colin letting him know he was off Missy duty for the day.

I wanted to find Bree Young. Even though Malone had talked to her, she had been with Betty when she found Mason's body. I had a few questions of my own. I had to start with the last place I'd seen her — Hot Handbags. Before I could talk with Quinn, I had to cover for Betty and her "personal errand."

I pointed the Jeep toward downtown. Traffic in the early afternoon was a bear. PCH crawled along. What would take only fifteen minutes in January, took almost twice that amount of time during peak tourist season.

While I was sitting in traffic, my cell rang. I answered using my hands-free.

"Hello?"

"Mel, it's Ella Johns. Did I catch you at a good time?"

"Of course." I watched a group of young surfers head toward Thalia Street Beach, surf boards in tow.

"I wanted to let you know I got the check. Thank you so much for dropping it off."

"Wonderful. We're only five thousand shy of our goal." The light turned green, and I drove toward the shop.

"Not anymore. And it's thanks to you. Nina Hernandez and Dash asked to be a sponsor. I was picking up her check when you dropped by."

God bless Nina. She was such a great supporter of all things animals. "Congratulations!"

"I wanted to celebrate reaching our goal. What about holding a small gathering to thank our major donors and sponsors?"

"What a great idea. Would you like to use the boutique?"

She laughed. "I was hoping you'd offer. I know this is really short notice, but I wanted to hold it on Saturday."

I almost jumped the curb. That was only four days away. I was thinking after I came back from Dallas. "That's awfully fast. Will we have time to get the word out? Will people come on such short notice?"

"The majority of them. I don't want to hold it too close to the event; otherwise people suffer from event exhaustion and won't come out to support the cause. I promise, if you provide the venue, I'll do everything else. I know Saturday is probably a busy day, so I was thinking we could do a brunch, around ten. You could open at noon."

"Of course. Anything for you and the dogs." This gathering was an excellent excuse to corral most of our murder suspects in one room.

"Mel, you're the best. I might have a special guest."

"Please don't say Sal Poochino."

A lusty laugh carried through the receiver. "No, no. He's semi-committed to the actual event. Unfortunately, Ms. Sweetin had a prior engagement, but is sending some memorabilia we can auction off."

"That's very generous."

"Isn't it? I've got to run. Thanks again for everything. I'll call you tomorrow with more details."

I suddenly had a wild idea. What if I added a few extra guests to our party? Like Grey. And maybe I'd let Betty invite her new boyfriend. I'd like to see Quinn and Leo in the same room. I had a feeling they were hiding a very important piece of their relationship from the rest of us. Maybe it was a link as to why Mason was killed.

I breezed into the shop. The afternoon sunlight brightened the space, filling it with a lazy warmth. It smelled like freshly brewed coffee. Betty must have replenished the breakfast blend I'd brewed earlier in the morning for our coffee bar. Complimentary coffee was always a hit with our customers.

"Sorry I'm a little late, Betty."

She wasn't paying any attention to my late arrival. She was too busy reprimanding a young man wearing a polo shirt and khakis. He held his black backpack defensively in front of him.

"Look, kid." She poked his backpack. "You don't know what you're talking about. If Cookie hired you, I'd know all about it. I'm her Girl Friday."

Darn, darn, darn. FBI Agent Tom James had beaten me to the boutique before I'd had an opportunity to prepare Betty. This undercover business was hard for someone with no training and no experience. Heck, what was I supposed to call him? I assumed FBI Agent Tom James wasn't an option. I rushed to where Betty and Agent James faced off in front of the interactive toys. She eyed him suspiciously, blocking his pathway of a quick escape. One look at Agent James in his laid-back attire, I had to believe there'd been a change in plans that I didn't know about. Time to improvise.

"Betty, I forgot to tell you we'll have an intern from the Future Entrepreneurs organization for a few weeks."

Agent Tom James stared wide-eyed at my self-proclaimed right-hand woman, having a hard time keeping his eyes off her icy-pink eyebrows. What kind of undercover operator couldn't hide a reaction to something as simple as lipstick eyebrows? This didn't bode well.

He was young. Black curly hair, dark eyes, and he lacked the typical polished "Tom Ford" professional look I'd come to associate with the FBI.

He dragged his gaze away from Betty and looked at me. Relief washed over his youthful face. "Hi, nice to see you again. Thanks for taking me at the last minute." Agent Tom James possessed the deepest bass voice I'd ever heard. I swear it felt like I'd just received a voice massage.

Thankfully he knew enough to play along to my improvisation on his cover. I wondered what he'd been told by his superior. Hopefully, more than I had.

Betty crossed her arms. "Don't let his voice fool you, Cookie. He's still a kid. There's not enough room for Tommy Boy here. We've got all the help we need."

I sighed. This was going to more difficult than I realized. "If you're referring to Grey, he had something come up and won't be able to spend as much time here as he hoped for a few days. So this all works out for the best."

"The best for who? You're not leaving him with me while you're dealing with your crazy family a thousand miles away. I didn't take this job to babysit."

"You won't be babysitting. He's perfectly capable of working in our boutique. Even fifteen-year-olds work retail. Sorry," I said to Agent James.

He frowned, obviously insulted at our assumption regarding his age. "I've had plenty of jobs."

She scoffed. "He's barely old enough to tie his own shoes."

Good thing he was wearing loafers.

"Does she always talk about people like they're not there?"

"All the time. You'll find it charming once you get used to it." I shoved my tote under the counter. I'd lock it in the office later. Right now it was more important to do damage control.

"Betty, I talked to Ella this morning, and she asked that we host an open house Saturday for the donors and sponsors of the film festival. It starts at ten so we'll need to be here at nine."

She huffed. "Good thing we keep our place in tip-top shape." She glared at Agent James as she spoke, her pronouncement of an organized environment for his benefit.

She wasn't wrong. We did keep a tidy boutique.

"Cookie, can I bring a plus one?"

I was sure she was talking about Leo.

"I've got my own boy toy now," she announced loudly, even though we were standing right in front of her. "I want to show him off."

"If you two will be spending time together, it's probably a good idea." I played it low key, not wanting to tip her off that I had my doubts about Lover Boy.

Agent James set his backpack on the floor. "Am I expected to attend, Ms. Langston?"

"Yes," I said, at the same time Betty said, "No."

I glared at her to keep quiet.

"Yes, you should be here. Okay, Tom, let's show you the ropes."

Betty pushed up the sleeves of her loud Hawaiian-print top. "I'll do it." She looked a little too eager to boss around our new intern.

"Don't you have somewhere to be?"

"I've got five minutes to lay down the Betty Law." She rubbed her hands together. "First things first, don't touch the cash register until I've reviewed your background check. Don't sell the pawlish; that's my turf. And the treat jars." She cocked her head and stared at him. "Change of plans. You're in charge of selling the treat jars. You have to sell at least three a week."

"Or?" he asked.

She frowned. "Or what?"

"If I don't sell three jars a week?"

She thought about it for a second. "You'll have to purchase one."

"Betty, you can't make him purchase unsold merchandise. If that worked, you would own thirty-five dog sweaters."

She had the grace to duck her head. "Fine. I take lunch at one thirty every day."

He checked his watch, which I recognized immediately as a high-end GPS navigation and activity tracker. It might have looked too expensive for a young entrepreneur intern in the Midwest, but here in Southern California it was a typical accessory. "It's one thirty-five."

She glared at him. "Are you a smarty pants?"

He shook his head, wide-eyed.

"Good. There's only room enough for one of those here." She hiked up her elastic-waist pants. "What hours you working?" she asked.

He looked at me. "I was hoping I could work the closing shift."

"That's fine." It was time for me to take control of what was happening at my boutique after hours. I believed a stakeout of the stakeout was in order. Before he got too comfortable, I continued, "I'll be here with you."

Betty laughed. "She got ya."

"You can put your backpack in the office. Then walk around the store and look at the merchandise. Get a feel for what we sell. I'll talk with you in a few minutes about which items are from local designers. There are a couple we like to hand sell."

"I'm outta here," Betty declared. "When I come back, we'll continue your training." After issuing her last order, she dashed out the door.

He waited until she was no longer in view through the front window. "Where is she going?" he asked, dropping the younger man persona.

"I have no idea. Maybe you could use your FBI super sleuth skills and find out for me."

"You shouldn't say that out loud. Someone could overhear. It's against regulations," he said stiffly.

Oh Lordy, this was going to be painful. I kept my eye on the door, watching for customers. "Look, before someone shows up, we need to set ground rules."

He cleared his throat. "That's not the way it works, Ma'am."

I ignored him. My shop, my rules. "First of all, if you want to use my shop as your base of operations, never call me 'Ma'am' again. Second, it's my store so, yes, there are ground rules. Under no circumstances is Betty to know what you're doing here. Stick with the intern cover; she believes it. You look way too young for her to believe you're Grey's overseas art broker. Besides that, you're not wearing a suit. Betty will call you out on your attire. Don't let her age fool you; she's persistent and nosey. If she thinks you're hiding something, she will make it her mission to uncover your secret. Next, Grey and I are back together so he may pop by occasionally before I leave for Texas in a week." The lie rolled off my tongue as if it were the truth. Our on-again-off-again status must have made it easier for me to fib. I was sure that was all there was to it.

Agent James tensed. "He's not supposed to be here. He can't participate in the case."

Ugh. Another rule follower. We were definitely going to butt heads. "Yes, we're aware. But as my . . ." I struggled for a label. Not finding one, I said, "What I call him doesn't matter. He won't talk about the case with you, so there's no need to worry should he happen to stop by. Besides, you'll be grateful when he's here. He keeps Betty occupied."

"I'll have to inform my superiors." He sounded unsure. The thought of keeping Betty out of his hair must have been appealing.

He not only appeared young, he struck me as inexperienced, even with that deep whiskey-aged voice. I narrowed my eyes. "How many cases have you worked on?"

He cleared his throat. "Counting this one?"

"Sure."

"One." He dared me to make fun of him.

I was wrong. We *were* babysitting. I couldn't believe they'd replaced a seasoned agent with a green agent.

I released a heavy sigh and led him toward the office to stow away his personal items.

"A few pieces of advice, if Callum Mac-Avoy, TV reporter for Channel 5, stops in the shop, do not talk to him. He's a rat fink and is only about climbing the career ladder. Always keep in mind he's a reporter, and no matter what he says, he doesn't play well with others."

"I see." He dropped his bag on the floor, then slid it under my desk with his foot.

I prayed he did see. "Betty was serious about the pawlish."

He nodded.

We headed back out front. "The best way to get along with my clients is to authentically engage with their pets. If you're fake for even a second, they'll know. You don't have to push the merchandise. The regulars know exactly what they want; the majority of tourists are just looking. If we're lucky, they may stumble across something they can't live without."

"Thank you for the tips." His sincerity surprised me.

"You're welcome. Since Grey was always here alone after hours, I'm assuming you'll do the same. Here's a key. Make sure you lock up when you leave."

He tucked the key in his pocket.

"Lastly, keep your firearm near you. I'm assuming they briefed you on local crime, but to reiterate, there have been a number of break-ins downtown after business hours. So far no one has been hurt, and nothing taken, but at some point it's likely to escalate."

"Do the local authorities have any leads?"

Before I could answer, the bell above the front door jingled, and in walked Nina and Dash. I excused myself from Tom and met Nina next to the gourmet treats.

"Hey there," I greeted her. I waited for

her kiss, kiss, but she only offered one before pulling away.

She must have been distracted by Agent James who hovered indiscreetly behind us. "Nina, this is Tom. He's interning for a few weeks. Tom, this is one of my favorite customers, Nina Hernandez, and her adorable dachshund, Dash."

He bent down and reached a hand out to Dash, who pranced in a circle. "Very nice to meet you."

Dash stopped moving long enough for a solid scratch behind the ears. Agent James then stood and bestowed a dazzling smile in Nina's direction. "It's a pleasure to meet you too, Ms. Hernandez."

Nina looked smashing in her pineapple-print romper and wedge sandals. She smiled back at Agent James, smoothing her long brown ponytail with freshly manicured fingers. "Nice to meet you too. Mel, can I talk to you for a second?"

"Sure. Tom, you're in charge. Why don't you show Dash the new chewy toys?" I led Nina toward the coffee bar. "I'd offer you some caffeine, but you seem on edge already. Are you okay?"

She squeezed the leather strap of her handbag. "You know I love Paws for Angels."

"I do. I'm sure Ella has already thanked you, but I'd like to thank you too. It's wonderful that you've offered to be a sponsor. Your donation is the reason we reached our goal."

"Right." She cleared her throat and looked around, obviously struggling to tell me something. "About that . . ."

I frowned when she didn't finish her sentence. "I know it's a large chunk of change. Don't worry; it's a tax write off."

"Yes, Ella mentioned that. Here's the deal. My accountant just informed me of a little hiccup," she rushed out.

"What kind of hiccup?"

"Well, I'm having a slight cash flow problem."

I schooled my expression hoping I didn't show my surprise. In the socioeconomic circles Nina ran, that was code for tittering on bankruptcy. "I'm sorry to hear. Do you need your check back?" I asked softly.

Nina looked like she was about to cry. "No, no. Can you just get Ella to hold the check for a few days? Evan said he'd have the situation corrected by Friday."

Evan? *The* Evan? "You employ the same bookkeeper as Mason and Quinn?"

She nodded. "They recommended him to me when my accountant, Paulie, retired a few months ago." She leaned close and whispered, "Paulie recommended his partner, but I'd heard through the grapevine that he was spending more time at the fat farm and the plastic surgeon than the office."

That didn't sound unusual for Orange County. "No kidding?"

She nodded. "I know, right? I wanted someone I could count on, and recognize."

"From the one interaction I had with Evan, he seems very thorough." I patted her arm. "Don't worry about it. I'll be very discrete."

Her tense shoulders relaxed as she released a heavy sigh. "I knew I could count on you. Thank you." She squeezed my hand.

"Of course."

"How are you? Any news on Mason's death?"

"Not much. The police are still waiting on the autopsy."

"Do they have any suspects? I heard about Callum MacAvoy's TV report. I hate to tell you, people are talking about it. It sounded like your ex could be involved."

I forced a smile. "Fake news. You know how MacAvoy is, always looking for the salacious angle on a story. Since you brought it up, I am curious. How often do you shop at the boutique?"

She shrugged. "Maybe once a month. I don't always buy something, but it's fun to look."

"I have a love affair with handbags myself. I was wondering if you knew Bree Young. Tall blond with a braid that hangs down to her waist. She shops at Hot Handbags, too."

She shook her head. "She doesn't sound familiar. I'm sorry. Is it important?"

"Don't worry about it."

I noticed Agent James and Dash stood behind me. I turned. By the look on his face — Agent James, not the dog — he'd been listening to our conversation. He was sharper than I wanted to believe.

"I found a jar of treats behind the counter. Do you care if I give one to Dash?" he asked Nina.

"Just one."

"Got it. Nice purse. It looks like something my mom would like."

I hated to admit it, but he found a smooth way to use his young looks to his advantage of putting people at ease as he secretly questioned them.

She smiled, surprised. She caressed her hazel tote. "Thanks. It's a recent splurge. You have a good eye. I just love Saint Laurent."

He looked confused. "Sorry, I'm not familiar with the saints. I'm protestant."

Nina suffocated a snicker. Her gaze darted in my direction.

"That's a French design house." I prayed his lack of designer knowledge was an act.

"Oh. Yes. Of course." He ran his fingers through his thick black hair. "Ms. Langston, I'd like to take a short break."

Hopefully it was to brush up on his designer brands. "Call me Mel. Be back in fifteen."

Once he walked away, Nina asked, "He's not from around here, is he?"

"How could you tell?" I was only half joking.

He was good with the animals, but if he was going to crack Grey's case at Hot Handbags, Agent James was going to need all the help he could get.

CHAPTER FOURTEEN

I managed to get Ella to hold Nina's check until the weekend by telling her the accountant cut it on the wrong account and that Nina would bring a different check to the party. Ella was none the wiser, and Nina was thrilled.

By three o'clock, Betty had returned with fresh pretzels, hot cheese, a large bouquet of flowers, and Leo. The food was her way of buttering me up to drop a bombshell. Leo had to be the grenade. The good Lord only knew when she would pull the pin. I prayed we had enough time to take cover.

Betty placed her flowers on the counter, front and center, so everyone could admire them.

Once Agent James had finished assisting a handful of customers, Betty quizzed him on the types of merchandise we carried, the proper way to answer the phone, how to make a sale, and finally, how many treat jars he'd sold.

"Isn't she a firecracker?" Leo asked with a besotted smile on his square face.

More like a nuclear bomb. "Looks like we'll be spending more time together now that you and Betty are . . . spending time together."

He adjusted the vase of flowers so they sat in a ray of sunlight. "Ah, yes. More opportunities to persuade you to expand the business."

"Is that what you were talking to Quinn about the other day? You offered to help her expand too?"

"Something like that." He watched Betty instruct Agent James on the proper way to hang the doggie tuxedos.

I held back from snapping my fingers in his face to get his complete attention. "Whatever it was you offered, she was adamant that she wasn't interested."

"She'll change her mind. She always does once she realizes what's in it for her." His shrewd smile put me on alert. "Mason and I had an agreement. I expect her to honor it. I just offered to sweeten the deal now that she's a widow."

I pressed for details. "Seems Mason was making all kinds of deals without his wife's knowledge. What did he agree to?"

"To sell me his business."

I didn't see that coming. Did Grey know? I fought the urge to look at Agent James. A better question would be, did Leo know about the counterfeit handbags? "Nothing in writing?"

"A man's word is binding."

"I see. Quinn doesn't seem the type to blindly follow secondhand information. In fact, she seemed to be in a good place for someone whose husband had just died." I wondered if he'd had the same opinion of their marriage as Evan.

He looked at me thoughtfully, weighing his words. "Yes, she does. She's, dare I say, happier."

Was he implying Quinn was glad her husband was dead?

"Cookie," Betty yelled across the room. I jumped.

"What?"

She stomped toward us. Here it was. The bomb.

"You've been holding out on me. Tommy Boy said you and Grey are officially an item again. I can't believe you told him before me, but I forgive you."

Well, crapola. This bomb was of my own making.

She wrapped her twiggy arms around my

227

waist and squeezed. "He obviously followed my advice. I knew it would work."

I wondered what advice she'd given Grey. I hugged her back, swallowing my guilt. It was one thing to lie to a complete stranger; it was another thing all together to lie to Betty. She was genuinely excited for us and felt she'd had a hand in orchestrating our reunion.

"Now, don't get too excited. We're still working things out." I felt the need to downplay the fake reunion.

She straightened her outfit and looked at Leo. "Wait until you meet Cookie's man. Hubba hubba. He's a catch."

"I'm looking forward to it. What does he do again?"

"He's famous," Betty bragged. "He owns ACT Gallery."

I rolled my eyes. "He's not famous."

Betty's gray eyes sparkled with mischief. "Now that you're back together, I guess that means I'm in charge." She puffed out her chest.

I sensed a train wreck in my immediate future. "What are you talking about?"

"When you two go to Texas to meet the baby." She narrowed her eyes in our intern's direction. "Don't you worry. I'll keep my eye on him."

Dang. I hadn't thought that through. Of course, everyone would assume Grey would accompany me. I immediately began digging out of the hole I'd created.

"We haven't talked about it. With the trip being such short notice, I'm not sure he can get away."

Plus the fact that he was a suspect in a possible murder; Malone may not want him to leave town. I crossed my fingers Grey would be in the clear by then.

Betty shook her finger at me. "What could be more important than joining you in Dallas to see your family? He wouldn't miss it for the world."

He would if I didn't invite him. How would I ever explain that? I prayed our fake reunion didn't get back to Dallas. Lord have mercy on my sinner's soul if my mama found out I'd been lying about me and Grey. There would be hell to pay.

I stepped next door hoping to catch Darby, but she wasn't in. I sent her a text and in the spur of the moment, walked up the street to Hot Handbags.

It seemed Quinn held the answers to many of my questions. Who was Leo, really? What, if anything, did Quinn know about Bree Young.

I walked inside the store and inhaled the enticing scent of expensive leather. The steady stream of customers that had been there a couple of days earlier had decreased significantly. It wasn't because the appetite for gossip had been satisfied. If I had to guess, it was because there wasn't a new scandal to buzz about. Give it time.

I didn't see Quinn right away. I took the opportunity to nonchalantly view the merchandise with a fresh eye. Even though it wasn't Grey's investigation, I wondered if there was anything I could make a note of to move it along a little quicker. It was hard to know what would be helpful when neither he nor Agent James had shared details.

Grey had mentioned that counterfeit purses were a booming industry and that it was difficult to intercept the products as they entered the country. Usually, it was easier to pinpoint counterfeits because they were priced significantly lower than the real purses. If the Reeds were dealing in counterfeit merchandise, they were expecting full price. I roamed the display case along the wall, checking price tags. All the prices were Laguna Beach appropriate.

I pulled out my phone and took a picture of an Alexander McQueen's skull clutch. I had one exactly like it in my closet. This one looked just like mine, but if I was ever able to tell if a handbag was counterfeit this would be the one.

I'd just taken the photo when Quinn asked from behind me, "What are you doing?"

My heart jumped into my throat. I fumbled my phone, almost dropping it. "I was telling a friend about this bag. I thought I'd take a photo so she could see what I was talking about."

"We don't allow photos. Delete it," she ordered.

I managed to calm my racing pulse. "I don't know why you wouldn't. The designer showcases his entire line on his website."

Her lips twisted disapprovingly. "Then find them there."

What was that saying? "The lady protests too much"? Made me believe she was hiding something. There was no way I was deleting that photo now. I set out to distract her from the photo.

"Your friend Leo has taken a liking to my associate, Betty."

"Really? The one with . . ." She touched her eyebrows. I nodded. A satisfied smile tugged at her lips. "Good, she can keep him out of my hair."

"That will be difficult if he's buying your store." I launched my own version of *Opera-*

231

She sucked in a breath. "Is that what he told you?"

I nodded. "Just a short time ago. He stopped by to see Betty."

Now we were getting somewhere. Heightened emotion could cause people to speak the truth before they had time to filter their thoughts.

"Well, that's not happening." She spun around and yelled toward the upstairs, "Evan! Get down here. Now."

I flinched at the animosity in her voice. I searched the store, watching the other customers. A couple of them stared in our direction, wide-eyed with curiosity. There was no way they'd leave anytime soon.

Evan ran down the metal stairs. He held his glasses in place as he rushed to Quinn's side. "What's wrong? What happened?"

"Have you found any paperwork supporting Leo's claim that Mason promised to sell him the store?"

He gulped and glanced at me before answering. "No, not yet."

"I knew it." Her green eyes sharpened with determination. "That's because there isn't anything. A verbal agreement with a dead man won't hold up in court. The store is mine."

232

I half expected a victorious cackle to explode from her mouth while thunder shook the building. The handful of customers who remained buzzed excitedly in hushed tones.

"If he comes in here again making these foolish claims, call the police and have him thrown off the premises," she ordered Evan.

Wow. Cold. Although if someone was trying to take my only means of making a living, I might sound eerily similar.

He adjusted his glasses. Beads of sweat formed on his forehead. "Sure thing." He turned to head upstairs. Quinn grabbed his arm and stopped him.

"About the other matter?"

He looked in my direction nervously. "You want to discuss this now?" he squeaked.

Her eyes widened as if she was attempting to silently communicate something of importance. "Yes, Evan. I want her out of my hair, too."

"Well, Mason decided he didn't want the painting anymore and wanted to return it."

"Yes, yes. You've already said that." She waved her hand, dismisssing the explanation. "But Mel has informed me that it came with an appraisal for insurance purposes. So why would Mason ask for another one?" She tapped her foot impatiently.

"Oh, I don't think that's true." Evan's voice cracked under the pressure.

Before I could refute this comment, Quinn said, "Grey Donovan is her ex. She should know how it works. Let me ask you again. Why did Mason want the appraisal?"

He cleared his throat. "Like I said, he decided not to keep it. He, ah, tried to sell it, but they told him it was a fake."

"Who told him that?" I asked. Why would Mason change his mind about owning the art piece two months after purchasing it?

"I'm not sure."

Quinn crossed her arms. "Hogwash. Mason ran everything past you. You know more about my financial situation than I do."

Judging from the intense scrutiny she was dishing Evan's way, that was about to change.

"Put the ledger and balance sheets on my desk within the hour. I'm going to review the books myself. I want to know exactly what's going on with *my* money."

Evan blanched. "I'd be happy to review the books —"

"I don't need you to audit the books. I'll do it myself. And trust me, if I find one penny missing, I'll be looking for an explanation."

Judging by Evan's expression, he had a lot

of explaining ahead of him. He skittered back upstairs.

With the drama over, the majority of customers scattered from the store, eager to report the happenings to their friends. We watched them scatter out the front door like cockroaches in the daylight.

Quinn gasped.

"Don't worry about it," I suggested in what I hoped was a helpful, concerned tone. "You can't control the gossiping. Give it a few weeks and a new scandal will become top news."

"I think I saw a ghost," she said in a hushed voice. Her unnaturally pale face worried me. Was she going to pass out?

"Maybe you should sit down," I suggested.

I followed her line of vision. A group of people dawdled outside the store, faces pressed against the window. I assumed they were looking at the purses, but judging by Quinn's bizarre reaction, I was wrong.

"Who did you see?"

She raced to the door and threw it open. With a loud gasp, the crowd backed away from the crazy lady. Good call on their end.

Quinn frantically looked in both directions. "Go away," she shouted. "Leave me alone."

Hell's Bells. Who had the power to scare Ice Queen Quinn?

CHAPTER FIFTEEN

The following morning, I met Darby at the Koffee Klatch at nine o'clock. We sat outside on the small patio facing PCH, enjoying the cloudless, blue sky and our morning caffeine. I breathed in the fresh salty air rolling off the ocean, energized to conquer the day.

A steady stream of people flowed along the sidewalk across the street toward downtown. Although the crowds were a mixture of locals and tourists, the locals were easy to identify by their dark tans and lack of beach arsenal.

I leaned back on the wrought-iron patio chair and turned my attention to my best friend. "You look fantastic this morning. Love the outfit."

Darby wore a cute canary-yellow maxi dress with white Keds sneakers. She'd tucked her blond curls under a straw hat that I wasn't sure how she managed to keep on her head. It was impressive. I felt a bit underdressed in my plain off-the-shoulder tee and skinny jeans.

She smiled. "Thanks. Have you replaced the boots Missy destroyed?"

"Not yet." I set my chai on the multicolored mosaic-tile table top. "Tell me about your breakfast date with Colin."

She grinned self-consciously. "First tell me why you were at Grey's house yesterday."

"How did you know about that?" I kept my voice light.

"How do you think?"

Loose Lips Betty, of course. I searched for the right words to describe my current relationship with Grey that were believable without lying to my best friend.

"With Grey spending more time at the boutique, Betty's been pushing us together. I guess her pain-in-the-butt efforts have sort of paid off. With so much history between us, we thought we'd try one last time to see if we could work things out."

She watched me cautiously. "That seems reasonable. And not exactly like you. But I like your thoughtful approach."

"Well, maybe I'm just maturing as a person." I laughed. "Okay your turn. What's going on between you and Colin? How was your breakfast date?"

Darby blushed. "It's going fine. The date was enjoyable."

I tossed a crumpled napkin across the table. "Oh, no, no, no. That is not good enough. I want details."

"Maybe later." She lowered her voice. "Any news on Mason's death?"

I sighed. "Grey is still a person of interest. I talked to Malone. He said the police are leaning toward Mason being pushed."

Her mouth formed a perfect O. "Betty was right." Her voice dropped to a hushed whisper.

"Good grief, don't tell her that. She's already difficult. Did she tell you about wanting to be a private investigator?"

"She's serious?"

I nodded. "Afraid so."

Over Darby's shoulder, I caught a glimpse of a very tall blond with a long braid swaying across her back on the opposite side of the street. I leaned forward for a better look.

Darby looked behind her. "What are you looking at?"

"It's her." I jumped up, the feet of my chair scraping the cement. "Come on."

She stood. "Who? Where are we going?"

I tossed my half-empty cup in the trash. "Amazon Barbie. I don't want her to get away." I took off in the direction I'd seen

Amazon Barbie walking, watching for a break in traffic.

Darby chased after me, one hand pressing her hat on her head, the other carrying her mocha latte.

We darted across the street, cars honking at us.

"Who's Amazon Barbie?" Darby asked, gasping for air as we weaved between people jogging up the street.

I didn't answer. I kept charging forward, pushing past the clusters of people. I jumped to the side as a young skateboarder whizzed past us. We'd raced about half a block when I realized I'd lost her. We stopped in front of a local liquor store.

Once I'd caught my breath, I explained. "She's the woman who was with Betty when Mason was found at the bottom of the staircase."

Darby looked confused. "Her name is Amazon Barbie?"

"That's what Betty called her, and it kinda stuck. Her name is actually Bree Young."

Darby tossed her empty cup into the trash can near the front door of the liquor store. "Why are we chasing her?"

"I wanted to talk to her."

"So you're going to chase her down the street? That's not creepy or anything."

I sighed. I was coming off rather desperate. Or crazy. I knew from past experience, Malone wouldn't consider Grey innocent until he found proof convincing him otherwise.

"Where do you think she disappeared to?" Darby asked.

"I don't know. Maybe into one of the businesses?"

We walked up the street another block, peering through each business's windows as we passed. We didn't find her.

Darby pulled off her hat and ran her fingers through her curls. "I don't see her."

That's when I saw the official Channel 5 News vehicle parked up the street in front of the Mediterranean bistro. *MacAvoy.* "Come on. I think I know where she is."

We power-walked to the restaurant. Without a second thought or a plan on what to say, I yanked open the door and stepped inside. It took a few seconds for my eyes to adjust to the dim lighting.

"Do you see MacAvoy?" I asked.

"Not yet."

Finally, I found them in the back of the restaurant, near the window facing the ocean. Bree Young and Callum MacAvoy sat at a four-person table, heads together, conversing. Mr. TV's dark chinos and white

241

polo shirt blended in to the crowded bistro. But the TV station's logo, proudly embroidered on the front of his shirt, had caught my eye.

"Gotcha, Mr. TV."

I grabbed Darby's hand and dragged her through the bistro toward them, never taking my eyes off the blond in teal-colored yoga pants and silver crop top. I pulled out the chair next to MacAvoy and sat down. Darby next to Bree.

I flashed my own version of a megawatt grin in the reporter's direction. "MacAvoy, imagine running in to you here."

He grunted, dismayed by our arrival. "Melinda. Darby. What are you doing here?"

"The same as you." I focused on Bree across the table. She was younger than I'd originally thought, maybe mid-twenties.

I waited for Mr. TV to make introductions. His fake tan must have killed off the brain cells managing his social graces. When he remained silent, I took matters into my own hands. "Hello, I'm Melinda. This is my bestie, Darby."

She smiled cautiously. "I'm Bree. You look familiar. Have we met before?" she asked me.

Darby eyed me. I knew what she was

thinking, that Bree had noticed us following her.

"Her ex-fiancé, Grey Donovan, is the prime suspect in Mason's murder." Mac-Avoy didn't waste any time throwing Grey and me under the bus.

She cocked her head. "No, that's not it." She tapped a finger on her bottom lip. "I remember." She pointed at me. "You were with that crazy old lady when we found Mason."

I wasn't offended. Next to Betty, everyone was forgettable. "And you disappeared before anyone could talk to you. Where did you run off to in such a hurry?"

She looked at me and then Darby. "I've already talked to the police."

MacAvoy rolled his eyes. "She fancies herself a private investigator of sorts."

"No more than you fancy yourself an investigative reporter."

Darby groaned.

I'd never win Mr. TV to my side if I baited him, but I didn't really need him on my side. I needed Bree.

Darby smiled at Bree. "Don't mind them. They haven't learned how to play well with each other yet."

A waitress stopped at the table with a coffee for MacAvoy and lemon water for Bree.

"So are you two on a date or is this an official interview?" I asked once the waitress left.

Bree stared wide-eyed at MacAvoy.

He ripped open two packets of sugar and dumped them in his mug. "It's really none of your business. Don't you have a dog collar to sell?" He grabbed a spoon to stir his coffee.

"You made it my business when you broadcasted a false story implicating Grey in a crime he did not commit."

He cocked an eyebrow. "He sent you to do his dirty work?"

"Really? That's what you think? You need to get your facts straight."

He swiveled in his chair to face me, blowing coffee breath in my face. "The fact is, Melinda, he was seen at the scene of the crime shortly before Mason was killed."

"That doesn't mean he entered the building or that he even spoke to Mason," I argued. "And how do you know your source is credible?"

MacAvoy's gaze flickered in Bree's direction. She squirmed in her seat.

I narrowed my eyes and studied the tall blond across from me. "You're his source? The person who was at the scene *when* the victim was found at the bottom of the stairs." I turned to the side and looked at MacAvoy, shocked. "Unbelievable. Simply unbelievable."

He shrugged. "She isn't protecting someone."

"You don't think she's protecting herself?" Darby's logical tone wasn't incriminating, yet it was very direct.

Bree waved her hands in the air getting our attention. "Hello, can I talk?" She cleared her throat. "Actually, Mr. MacAvoy, that's why I wanted to meet you."

All eyes turned to her.

She looked uncomfortable. "Now that I've had time to reflect, I don't think it was Grey Donovan I saw." Her apologetic tone didn't appease MacAvoy.

His face turned red. "What?"

She pulled a folded piece of paper from her purse and slipped it across the table. "I think it was him."

MacAvoy, not pleased by the turn of events, grudgingly accepted the paper and unfolded it. I gasped. It was a picture of Colin from his Dog Days website. My head snapped up, and I looked at Darby.

"Are you sure?" MacAvoy and I asked at the same time. He looked as confused as I felt.

"What's wrong, Mel?" Darby bit her bottom lip.

I grabbed the paper from MacAvoy's grip and slipped it to Darby. She took one look, and all the blood drained from her face.

"I-I don't understand." Her gaze bounced between the three of us.

"Do you know him?" Bree asked.

"These two obviously do." MacAvoy yanked Colin's photo back from Darby. "You're sure this is who you saw?"

"Yes. He was outside Hot Handbags the morning Mason was killed," Bree stated with conviction.

"No. That's not true," Darby exclaimed.

"How do you know him?" MacAvoy asked again.

I was all kinds of confused. Colin and Grey looked nothing alike. Sure, they were both tall and handsome, but that was where the similarities ended. Grey had dark hair, Colin sandy blond. Grey had an athletic build, Colin slender. Grey had a sexy, dangerous edge to him. Colin was . . . nice.

I ignored Mr. TV's question and fell back to one of my original arguments. "You can't suspect everyone who passes by the store. We don't even know if they knew each other."

"But they did," Bree insisted, her voice

rising. "Colin had some type of information Mason wanted."

Darby knocked over Bree's glass. Cold water rushed across the table, straight for MacAvoy. He jumped up, mumbling something under his breath. My guess was that it wasn't suitable for broadcasting.

I quickly pulled a handful of napkins from the metal container and sopped up the mess. How did Bree know Colin? I studied Darby from under my lashes as I dried off the table. She looked shell-shocked.

"I'm so sorry," Darby muttered. She grabbed her own pile of napkins and handed them to Mr. TV.

"Don't worry about it," I reassured her. "Accidents happen." I piled the sopping napkins at the end of the table. Looking at Bree and her insistence that Colin had something Mason wanted, I realized she was more than a loyal Hot Handbags customer. She had to have known Mason on a more personal level.

"How do you know all of this? How well did you know Mason?" I asked.

She shrugged one shoulder. "As well as any other customer, I suppose."

I shook my head. "No. I have loyal customers, too. They don't know intimate information about my life. Just trivial gossip."

"If you don't mind, this is my meeting." Mr. TV glared at me.

If I believed he was competent to uncover the truth, I'd let him ask the questions. But his goal and my goal were at odds. I wanted the truth; he wanted ratings.

I pulled out my phone and snapped a quick photo of Bree.

"Hey," she screeched. "What are you doing?" She smoothed the sides of her hair then pulled her rope braid over her shoulder. Too late to primp now, sweetheart.

"I can easily confirm with Quinn if you're really a loyal customer by showing her this photo of you."

MacAvoy looked impressed with my quick thinking. Bree, on the other hand, looked terrified.

I rattled off a litany of questions. "So let's try this again. How are you connected to Mason? Why were you with Betty at the scene when he was found? And why did you leave so abruptly? Did you push him down the stairs?"

Bree's bottom lip trembled; her eyes filled with unshed tears. My barrage of questions was too much for her. She broke down. "No. I loved him," she burst out.

I looked at MacAvoy. This was all news to him. He frantically jotted notes. Where was his fancy voice recorder?

"You were having an affair?" Darby clarified.

Bree nodded. "He was leaving Quinn."

That would explain why he'd sell the store to Leo. It seemed Quinn was right, and Mason was hiding assets from her.

MacAvoy looked up from his notes. "Back to this information Colin had, what was it?"

She shrugged. "Mason never said. Just that Colin was a ghost from his past that he wanted gone once and for all."

Ghost from the past? Wasn't that what Quinn had whispered yesterday right before she ran outside like a lunatic yelling into the crowd?

CHAPTER SIXTEEN

I texted Betty that I'd be in late. She assured me everything was under control. Her version of under control and mine were vastly different, but at the moment I didn't have much of a choice.

Darby was more quiet than normal on the walk back to the coffee shop where we'd left our cars. I knew she was preoccupied thinking about Bree's accusation about Colin. I glanced at my best friend who walked next to me.

"If Bree is telling the truth, and she was having an affair with Mason, everything she says is suspect. She could be making it all up as a cover for herself."

Darby stared straight ahead. "I know. But it's obvious she's telling the truth about Colin knowing Mason. Why wouldn't he have said something? Mason's death has been all over the news, and he didn't mention once that he knew him. Doesn't that sound like he's hiding something to you?"

Well of course it did, but I didn't want to admit it to her. It was also possible he wasn't hiding anything and Bree had misconstrued the whole situation. Possible, but the probability was marginal at best.

"Are you going to talk to him?"

She glanced at me and caught my eye. "Of course."

I wanted first crack at dragging answers out of Colin, but it was only fair that as his girlfriend, Darby should interrogate him first.

I elbowed her. "If you'd like back-up, you know where to find me. Remember, if we find out he's guilty of something, I did promise him I'd make him pay if he hurt you."

She chuckled half-heartedly. "I remember."

Once we arrived back at the Koffee Klatch, we parted ways. I headed to the boutique and Darby to her studio. She promised to call once she'd talked to Colin.

When I entered the shop, the scent of lemon furniture polish competed with the aroma of freshly brewed coffee. Agent James, who was wearing cargo pants and a dark green t-shirt, was on his knees dusting the wooden shelves that stored the dog vests. I smiled. Poor guy. I'm sure that wasn't how he imagined his first undercover case would unfold.

Betty stood on a small stepstool cleaning the fingerprints off the glass display case. True to her word, Betty had it all in hand, ruling with an iron fist.

She looked up as I entered. "Cookie, it's about time you got here. That sexy detective was looking for you."

It's never a good sign when the homicide detective seeks you out two days in row. I pulled my cell phone out of my bag and set it on the counter next to the register. "Is he coming back?"

"He said he'd find you."

Oh, I was sure he would. I stashed my handbag in the office. I noticed Agent James had left his backpack under the desk. I resisted the urge to look inside. I hurried out of the room before I gave in to temptation.

I grabbed the can of furniture polish from Agent James. "Looks great. Can you make sure the coffee bar is stocked? In fact, I think we might need to pick up more to-go cups. Can you check in the storeroom?"

"Of course." He brushed off his pants then headed toward the back.

"Betty, where's the organic polish I

brought in last week?"

"That was junk. I've been using this brand for fifty years, and I ain't dead yet."

I sighed. Furniture polish wasn't worth fighting over.

My cell rang. Before I could reach for it, Betty glanced over and looked at the caller ID. She started making kissing noises.

"Stop," I said, knowing immediately it had to be Grey.

I grabbed it before Betty decided to answer it for me. No telling what she'd say or commit me to.

"Hey, there."

"I'm bored." Grey's voice drifted through the receiver. "I can't sit around and do nothing. Would you like to have an early dinner?"

I couldn't help it; I laughed. "Wow, that's a flattering invitation."

"Sorry, that didn't come out right." I could image him pacing along his back deck, coffee in one hand, rubbing his neck in frustration with the other hand.

I looked over my shoulder. Betty propped her elbows on the counter, her face resting in the palms of her hands, blatantly eaves-dropping.

I glared at her. She smiled, not moving an inch.

"I have a new intern. Tom James." I sounded more chipper than normal. I hoped he would understand what I was trying to say.

"You're not alone?"

"Betty's making sure I don't hang up on you."

"What about James?"

"Oh, you know how those young interns are. Would rather spend their mornings surfing than working."

I could see him rubbing his face in exasperation. "That's the second time you said 'intern'. Has there been a change in plans?"

"Sort of." I eyed Betty who closed her eyes and puckered her lips.

"Are you telling me he is inexperienced?" Grey asked.

"Exactly."

"I'm going to get drunk."

I chuckled. "No you're not. Darby and I learned a few things I want to run past you. Where do you want to meet for dinner?"

Betty straightened. "We should double date."

I shook my head.

"Party pooper," she huffed.

"I thought I'd pick you up." Grey's bland tone didn't fool me.

My stomach tightened. I wanted my own

wheels, in case I needed to make a hasty exit. "Let's meet. How about Charlie's Place at six?"

"I'll see you then."

The next six hours were going to feel like a lifetime.

Betty needed to run her personal errand at the usual time. Unlike Grey, Agent James took frequent breaks. I had a feeling they were case related. Betty thought he had a prostate problem and needed to be seen by a doctor.

I sent Agent James to pick up coffee bar supplies. He seemed happy for the excuse to get out of the shop. I had to give him credit. He had quickly become a hit with my customers. Maybe the bureau knew what they were doing after all.

Colin sent me a collection of photos of him and Missy. Not driving home to confront him about Mason killed me. But I told Darby I'd let her talk to him first. I would keep my word.

The afternoon dragged. Every time I caught myself thinking about dinner with Grey, I made myself donate one hundred dollars to the ARL. They were about to receive a hefty donation.

The boutique experienced a large amount

of traffic throughout the afternoon, but not much sold merchandise left the store. Everyone wanted to know the latest scoop on Mason's death. Since Betty and I had been involved in previous homicide cases, people assumed we had the inside information.

At five o'clock, Betty skipped out the door. I dropped off the bank deposit and then drove home to get ready for dinner with Grey. I reprimanded myself for being excited, but my heart wasn't listening.

In the words of a popular pop song, the heart wants what the heart wants.

CHAPTER SEVENTEEN

I took more care getting ready for dinner than I wanted to admit. As much as I told myself this was nothing more than comparing notes and filling him in on his replacement, that didn't stop the butterflies. I didn't want to overdress, but I wanted to look good. I finally decided on a navy-blue jumpsuit with a wrap bodice. Then I slipped on a pair of toffee-colored ankle strapped heels.

I left my hair down, allowing it to fall over my shoulders, and I applied minimal makeup — a swipe of mascara and tinted lip gloss.

I checked the finished look in the full-length mirror. Oh! One last very important item. I pulled my Alexander McQueen's skull clutch out of the closet. I'd compared the two and didn't find any dissimilarity. I wasn't sure the photos I'd taken at Hot

Handbags would be of use, but it was worth a try.

I made sure Missy had fresh water and tossed her a couple of dried apples. After she demanded an extra belly rub and scratch behind the ears, she trailed off to her bed.

I gingerly climbed into the Jeep, then made my way toward the restaurant, purposely keeping my mind from drifting to the past. Within fifteen minutes, I had arrived. Six o'clock on the nose. I walked inside and spied Grey, a relaxed smile on his face. Some things would never change, and his promptness was one of them.

He'd worn my favorite indigo poplin shirt that set off his blue eyes, paired with charcoal-colored trousers. My favorite look — sexy and dangerous.

His eyes locked on mine. I felt my cheeks warm.

"You're beautiful." His voice sounded calm compared to the jumble of emotions I was experiencing.

I smiled slightly. "You clean up pretty good yourself."

"No more three-day bender?" His eyes twinkled with humor.

I winced. "That was a bit harsh. Sorry about that."

He kissed my cheek lightly and whispered

in my ear, "In case anyone is watching."

My smile faltered. "Of course."

The hostess called our name and swept us off to our table through the well-lit dining room humming with relaxed chatter and soft background music. Charlie's Place was the quintessential Laguna experience. Local art hung on the walls, next to collectable photographs of old Hollywood celebrities. The staff, friendly and warm. Amazing food without emptying your wallet. A local favorite when a lovely and unique experience was on the menu.

Ever the gentleman, Grey assisted me with my chair before sitting himself. The hostess handed each of us a menu and then returned to her post at the front of the bistro.

"Do you need to look at the menu, or should we get our usual?" Grey asked, a glimmer of adventure in his eyes.

Could it still be your usual if you hadn't eaten it in over a year? I laid my menu at the edge of the table, accepting the challenge. "I'm always up for fondue."

Our waitress arrived with a complimentary bread basket, the yeasty smell tantalizing my nose. My stomach growled. Once we placed our order, our waitress left to fetch our cocktails. She returned a short time later with our drinks. Red wine for me,

Scotch for Grey.

I picked at the white table cloth, working hard to tune out the tension flickering between us.

Ice cubes cracked against the glass as Grey sipped his Scotch. "Tell me about Agent Tom James."

I filled him in on what had happed, including the day's events with Mr. TV and Bree Young, while he sipped his drink.

I wrapped up with my thoughts about Colin. "I think he's hiding something. I always have."

He studied me closely. "You've been busy."

"I've been lucky. I'll have to talk to Malone tomorrow. He stopped by the shop today before I arrived."

Grey waved over the waitress to bring us a couple of glasses of water. "He's not going to be happy with you."

I scoffed. "I'm used to it by now. I don't have any hard evidence, but I do have information he can follow up on. Oh, speaking of information . . ." I pulled out my cell and opened the photo app.

I pushed aside his tumbler, making room for my handbag. "Now, don't get upset. I took a photo of a purse at Hot Handbags. It's the same style as the one I'm carrying right now. This is the real deal. I thought maybe you'd like to compare the two." I handed him my phone. "I don't see any differences, but I don't know what I'm looking for."

He thoroughly compared the two before handing my phone and bag back to me. "It's hard to tell, but from what I can see, Quinn has an original."

"Darn."

"Don't let on to Agent James —"

"Have more faith in me than that." I cut him off before he said something offensive and ruined the night.

Our veggie and meat plates arrived first, followed by a large pot of piping-hot Gruyere cheese. We chatted easily about my trip to Dallas and my mama. What it would be like to see my baby niece. We talked about his most recent trip to New York where he attended an art auction and had bought a number of fabulous pieces he thought I'd like.

I recounted Betty's crazy flirting with Leo and how Leo seemed to be knee deep in the drama at Hot Handbags. Grey listened intently, but never gave away if I was telling him anything he didn't already know. I appreciated that he didn't tell me to keep my nose clean or attempt to change the subject.

I was in the middle of a Quinn story when he placed his hand on top of mine, the warmth of his touch effectively stopping me mid-sentence.

He smiled softly. "She's right behind you. Don't turn around."

I blinked, concentrating on what he'd said. I pulled my hand back and fluffed my hair. "Is she alone?"

"At the moment." To the other diners, it would seem Grey was gazing into my eyes, hanging on my every word. In reality, I knew there was an internal debate happening. He finally came to a conclusion. "How do you want to handle it?"

The knowledge that he'd made a conscious choice to not only work with me, but to ask my opinion, was exhilarating. "I guess it depends. I can take you to her table and introduce you, making her feel cornered. Or I could get up to use the restroom and bring her here to introduce you, making it her idea while giving her the sense of easy escape."

He nodded with a smile. "Go get her."

I set my napkin on the table and excused myself. I felt lightheaded as I walked toward Quinn. I was sure it was the wine and had nothing to do with Grey's trust in me.

Quinn, dressed in a bright-red pantsuit

and strappy heels, had her head down, frantically texting on her phone.

"Hello," I greeted her.

She lifted her head, her eyes suddenly suspicious. "Are you following me?"

I pointed to where Grey sat alone. "No, we've been here a while. I was just on my way to the restroom when I saw you on your phone."

She frowned. "Is that Grey Donovan? I thought you two weren't an item anymore?"

I shrugged. "We're going to give it one more try. Too much history and all that." The lie no longer felt like deception. I pushed that thought aside. Maybe I'd unpack it later to examine what that meant, but not now. For now I had to focus on Quinn. "I guess we have you and Mason to thank. Your whole ordeal is what pushed us together."

She mulled that over. "Introduce us." She started toward Grey.

I blocked her pathway. "I don't know if that's a good idea. If you're going to yell at him, I don't think I want you to talk to him." I crossed my arms. I couldn't make it too easy for her; she had to work for it.

She lifted her chin. "I'm not a hooligan."

I pretended to consider it. "Fine, but if you cause a scene, I'll call the cops." I led her to the table. "Look who I ran in to. Grey, this is Quinn Reed. Mason's wife. Quinn, this is Grey."

He stood and offered his hand. "It's a pleasure. I'm so sorry about your husband. Would you like to join us?" He pulled out a chair for her.

She studied him with a stiff smile. "Did you kill my husband?"

I gasped. I hadn't expected her to ask that right out of gate.

Grey remained standing. "No." He didn't elaborate. Just a plain simple no.

Whatever test that was, he passed. Quinn accepted the chair. She crossed her legs. "I'm meeting someone so I don't have much time. But I would like to ask a question."

"Of course," Grey said. "Would you like some wine while you wait for your companion? I'm sure we can get another glass."

She sniffed as if wine was beneath her. "I don't drink."

I was miffed that she came at Grey like that, but I reeled in my irritation and leaned toward Quinn, offering a sympathetic smile. "I was telling Grey earlier about what happened yesterday. You looked like you were about to faint. Are you feeling better?"

She brushed the whole incident off. "It

264

was nothing."

"Are you sure? You said you thought you saw a ghost. I have to tell you, you looked like you'd seen one."

She avoided my gaze. "It must have been my imagination playing tricks on me." She turned her attention to Grey. "I'd like to know more about this art transaction between you and my late husband."

He nodded solemnly. "I'll tell you what I can."

"Once Mason bought the painting, did he take it with him?" she asked.

"No, he wanted it delivered to his home." Grey spoke in a purposeful tone, leaving no room for misunderstanding.

Quinn pursed her lips. "Do you recall what address that was?"

He shook his head. "Not off the top of my head. I might recognize the street name."

"We're in Temple Hills, on Mar Vista Way."

"I'm sorry. I haven't delivered a piece to that area in a long time."

"I see," she murmured.

"I don't. If he didn't have it delivered to your store or to your home, where did he have it sent to?" I asked, genuinely perplexed.

She bristled. "I believe to our bookkeeper. Mason was hiding it from me. The crook."

I blinked back my surprise at her disgust.

"Could he have wanted to surprise you with a gift?" Grey asked.

"It possible," she conceded. "He could be rather romantic." She swung her crossed leg. "It's been years since he's surprised me with anything that significant."

Watching Quinn's body language, I thought about Bree's claim that she and Mason were in love, and that he was leaving his wife. Maybe he was romancing a new lady love. That led me to an uncomfortable thought. What if Colin and Quinn were past lovers?

I shifted in my chair. "Quinn, I learned we have another mutual friend."

"Oh," she sounded distracted.

"Colin Sellers. My dog sitter. Young, brownish-blond hair. Very good-looking."

Quinn's leg froze mid-swing. She tried desperately not to react, but she failed miserably. "I don't think I know him. I don't have a dog."

"He said he knew you and Mason. I think he mentioned talking to Mason just last week." I continued digging, using the information Bree shared.

"He did?" she sounded scared.

That wasn't the reaction I was expecting. Why could she possibly be afraid of Colin?

I exchanged a confused look across the table with Grey. My phone vibrated in my handbag. I ignored it. Whoever it was would leave a message.

"He's also dating my best friend, Darby Beckett, a photographer. She owns Paw Prints Photography."

"I said I don't know him," she snapped. She stood abruptly.

The diners at the table next to us paused their conversations and gawked in our direction.

"I'm sure my dinner companion has arrived." Quinn rushed off without a backward glance in our direction.

"That was telling." I pulled out my cell to see if the caller had left a voicemail.

"She knows Colin." Grey pushed Quinn's chair up to the table.

"I agree. But why deny it? Was she afraid, or am I reading that into her reaction? I can't help myself from wondering, but is it possible Quinn and Colin were . . . intimate?" I screwed up my face, disturbed by the possibility.

"Anything is possible. Don't discount it until you can rule it out."

My phone rang again. "It's Darby."

"It must be important. You better get it."

I silently agreed. "Hey Darby, what's going on?"

"Are you still with Grey?" Her panicked voice surprised me.

I shot a worried look at him. "I am. I'm going to put you on speaker phone." I turned my phone volume down so our private conversation wasn't broadcasted throughout the room. "What's wrong?"

"Colin's been taken in for questioning about Mason's murder."

Grey and I stared at each other. I was at a complete loss for words.

"Where are you?" Grey took over the conversation.

"The police station. Detective Malone is with him right now."

"We're on our way. Stay put." Grey gently took the phone from my hand and ended the call. "Let's go." He pulled out his wallet and left a pile of cash on the table.

I grabbed my purse and stood. I finally found my voice. "Sure wish you would have run that background check like I asked you to."

CHAPTER EIGHTEEN

The Laguna Beach police station was quiet at nine o'clock at night. Darby sat on the edge of her hard plastic chair straight from the eighties. Her shaky hands clutched the canvas shoulder bag in her lap. I sat next to my devastated best friend in silence. Grey stood in front of us, hands in his pant pockets.

"What happened?" Grey asked gently.

I wrapped my arm around Darby's shoulders, offering support.

"I went to confront Colin this evening about what Bree said about him. While I was at his house, Detective Malone showed up." She shuddered.

"Why?" I asked.

"I guess MacAvoy went to Malone this afternoon and spilled everything Bree said about Colin." Her voice quivered as she told her story. She took a deep breath and looked at Grey. "I guess Malone ran a background check on him."

"Did he?" Imagine that. I shot some major side-eye in Grey's direction.

He returned my look with one of his own that screamed, "Not now."

I almost didn't want to ask, but I did anyway. "I take it they found something suspicious?"

She nodded. "He's Mason's stepson," she said on a hiccup.

You could have knocked me over with a feather. "Holy cow. Why not just admit that when he arrived?" Not to judge, but he didn't seem too upset about Mason's death.

Darby let out a shaky sigh. "I don't know all the details, but from what Colin was able to tell me, he believes Mason murdered his mother years ago, but her body was never found. Last month was the twentieth anniversary of her death. Colin tracked Mason here. He just wanted to know the truth once and for all."

Hell's Bells. This was bad. No, this was worst-case scenario. I didn't have to be in Malone's position to see how a confrontation between the two men could easily turn into a shoving match. Colin accidently pushing his stepfather down the stairs in anger.

I struggled for something to say. "I guess

Mason's death was officially ruled homicide."

Something caught Grey's attention. He shifted his gaze toward the hallway. "Malone," he warned under his breath.

My stomach sank. His appearance wasn't a good sign. Detective Judd Malone had perfected the expressionless face. I had no idea what he was feeling or thinking, but I could safely say he was not excited or even happy to see us.

He stopped next to Grey. "Donovan. Melinda." I wouldn't call it a greeting, more like an acknowledgment that we were breathing the police station's air.

Grey nodded. "Detective."

Malone wore black jeans and a black t-shirt. Was that all he owned? I'd love to take a sneak peek in his closet.

Darby sprang to life. She jumped to her feet. "He didn't kill him."

Malone almost looked sorry for her. "You should go home. Mr. Sellers will be here a while."

She shook her head. "I'm staying."

"MacAvoy is on his way," the detective warned us. A flicker of compassion flashed across his stone face.

I nodded my thanks for looking out for Darby. He certainly didn't need to. Malone spoke in hushed tones with Grey. Both men were all business.

I tore my attention away from them and focused on my friend. "Darby, you hardly know Colin." I lowered my voice.

Her small frame vibrated with determination. "We have a lot in common, don't you think? You hardly knew me, but when I was accused of killing Mona, a mother I'd never met until moving here, you stood by me."

That was a different time. A different homicide. "It's not the same."

"Why not?" she demanded.

I rubbed my face. For one thing, not once did I think she was hiding a Texas-sized secret. Truth be told, in the back of my mind, I always felt Colin was hiding something.

Malone left. I assumed he returned to questioning Colin.

It was time for my best friend to face some hard truths. "If it wasn't Colin, then who?" I asked. "Because right now, he has the best motive in the world."

"That's what I need your help in figuring out." Darby's pleading blue eyes broke my heart. "He did stop by Hot Handbags, but he swears Mason was already dead."

I looked at Grey, who'd been silent during the majority of the conversation, for help. "I have to agree with Mel. He has a strong motive. Does he have an alibi for earlier in the morning?"

"He was walking Goose."

"Goose?" he asked with a raised brow.

"His dog," I said.

"Did he talk to anyone? A neighbor, business owner?" God bless Grey; he was trying.

She shook her head.

I sighed. "I'm not sure what we can do, but we'll do what we can. Right, Grey?"

The look he gave me was not encouraging.

I grabbed Darby's hand and squeezed. "Betty's going to be beside herself when she finds out we were at the police station without her."

Grey followed me home around eleven that night. I invited him inside to talk about Darby's situation and what, if anything, we could do to help her. My head was still spinning with the late evening's events. I poured us each a glass of wine to unwind.

We sat on the couch in the dim table lamp lighting. Missy curled up between us, snoring, not a care in her doggie world. A comfortable silence surrounding us as we contemplated Darby and Colin.

"What do you think?" I grabbed a throw pillow and tucked it behind my back for support. Now that the excitement was over and the wine warmed my body, I realized I was exhausted.

Grey stretched out his long legs. "It's a good sign that Malone didn't arrest him. That means he's still building his case."

"But it sounds like it's a going to be a solid case."

He shrugged. "No case is perfect. But Malone is a good detective."

I set my wine on the end table. I hopped up from the couch and grabbed the notepad and pencil from the junk drawer in the kitchen. I returned to the living room and dropped to the couch.

"Okay, let's review. We have a handful of suspects: Colin, the stepson; Bree, aka 'Amazon Barbie,' the mistress; Quinn, the not-so-grieving widow; Evan, the bookkeeper; and Leo, the businessman."

Grey smiled. "Thanks for leaving me off the list."

"You were never on it."

He shifted his position to face me. Missy opened one eye and snorted her objection. He patted her head and told her to go back to sleep.

"If we take Colin off the list, who has the

strongest motive?" I asked.

"All of them," Grey stated.

We studied the suspect list. I wrote the words "Love or Money" and underlined them twice.

"The motive is either love or money," I said.

"Probably," he agreed.

I'd place my money on love every time.

CHAPTER NINETEEN

I woke up early the next morning. That would be around seven for me. After the night before, I needed to start the day with a clear head, so I took a short run on the beach before the sunburned tourists dominated the popular destination. I soaked up the sunshine as my feet pounded the wave-packed sand. I concentrated on the rhythm of my stride, blocking out all other thoughts. One thought I wasn't able to banish was that I didn't have a dog sitter anymore. Colin had to concentrate on clearing his name.

Once home, I ate a banana and some Greek yogurt. Missy demanded a few dried apple slices of her own. I grabbed a quick shower and dressed comfortably in a pair of black leggings and a silver asymmetrical tunic. I swiped on some mascara and lip gloss. Finally ready for the day, I kissed Missy on the head, slipped on a pair of flats, and headed to the shop.

It was during the crawl down PCH in the morning beach traffic that I had a brilliant idea. I'd call Evan Dodd to schedule an appointment with the bookkeeper. It was time to figure out exactly what he knew and if he was covering for Mason. But first I had a few special orders to place, and I wanted to call my mama. I noticed she'd left a couple of voicemails during my run. I knew from experience, if I waited too long to return her call she'd not only keep calling, but she'd send in reinforcements.

I arrived at the shop around nine thirty, the first one in for the day. I booted up the computer and opened the register. There were no messages requiring a response, so I quickly made my calls. Evan wasn't in yet, but his answering service was able to schedule an appointment at eleven. Mama had called to inform me she'd registered Elmsly at a Dallas high-end boutique. Mama was on and off the phone in record time.

Betty rolled in wearing a new purple satin muumuu with a lace collar at precisely ten o'clock, a solid hour before we opened.

She stowed her straw handbag in the office then rushed back to the coffee bar. I'd started a fresh pot after my phone calls.

She sniffed the air. "Smells strong. What

are you doing here so early, Cookie?" Betty poured herself a mug full of the strong brew and tasted it.

"Just wanted to get a jump on the day."

"I bet. I heard about all the excitement last night." She wiggled her mocha-brown eye brows. They almost looked normal. Almost.

"There was more waiting around than thrills." I downplayed the drama.

"But I heard we're conducting our own investigation now that Grey's off the hook and the Dog Whisperer is the prime suspect." She slapped out her investigator's notebook next to the creamer. "I've been doing a little digging for a while."

I picked up the notebook and handed it back to her. "Is that where you've been disappearing to every afternoon?"

"Not that it's any of your business, but no. That's a whole new project." She tucked the notebook under her arm.

I was afraid to ask but couldn't stop myself. "What project?"

She grabbed her mug. "You'll just have to wait and see."

"I can't wait." My sarcasm was as thick as week-old coffee.

She shuffled to the counter. She tossed

her notebook down and set her cup on top of it.

"My flowers still look beautiful." She stuck her nose in the middle of the blooms and inhaled deeply. "They smell heavenly. How do you think our sexy detective will take it when I tell him I have a boyfriend?"

Relieved? "I'm sure he'll get over it in time."

"I'll make sure to let *all* the fellows down gently. I am a hard habit to break, ya know." She cocked her hip and batted her eyes.

The front door opened, and in sauntered Mr. TV.

"Who left the door unlocked?" I asked, immediately irritated by the arrival of our uninvited guest.

"That was you, Cookie," Betty cackled. "It was unlocked when I got here."

Damn.

"Ladies." His rich TV-ready voice needlessly broadcasted his arrival. He made an effort to impress today, dressed in his business casual outfit with sport coat.

"No need for dramatics. It's just me and Betty." I rolled my eyes. If only everyone else loved him as much as he loved himself, he might actually have a decent-sized fan club.

Betty raced toward him and stopped him.

"I have some bad news."

He looked at me, silently asking for help. I shook my head. "You entered on your own free will. You get what you get."

He shoved his hands in the front pockets of his black chinos. "Mrs. Foxx, what bad news?"

She grabbed his bicep and squeezed. "I got me a sugar daddy."

He blinked. "You do?"

She patted his chest over the sport coat he wore. "I know it's hard, but you'll have to move on. I'm a faithful woman so you'll have to turn your attention elsewhere. And Cookie's back with her handsome man, so she's not available either."

"Well, I'm devastated to hear that you've been taken off the market. He must be an interesting fellow."

"That he is," I interjected before Betty spilled all the happenings here at the shop, like the arrival of our newest intern.

"What can I do for you, MacAvoy? I'm sure you're not here to purchase a dog costume for next month's event."

Betty slid behind Mr. TV and patted his butt. He jumped ten feet. "Hey, that's harassment," he yelped.

"He's clean, Cookie. I patted him down. No recorder." She brushed her hands together proud of herself. "Whatever we say here is off the record, got it?" she glared at him.

I held back my appalled laughter. "Betty, you can't go around touching people inappropriately. If he'd done that to you, you'd be upset."

She eyed him. "Did I offend you?"

He kept his backside away from her. "You surprised me."

"See, he's just fine."

"Listen, MacAvoy. Lately, it seems when you're around, I have three speeds: on, off, and don't push your luck. We open soon, and I don't want you loitering here when my customers arrive. You've got two minutes. Go."

"Is she right, you're back with Donovan?"

I didn't understand why it mattered to him or why my reunion with Grey made him cranky. "Surely, you came here for something more important than an update on my personal life."

"I'm running a story on Colin Sellers."

"Of course you are. Haven't you done enough?" I crossed my arms to keep myself from reaching for him.

"Shouldn't you be thanking me now that Donovan is no longer a suspect? Now that you're back together." The last sentence was spoken as if it left a bad taste in his mouth.

"That's your problem. You have lousy logic."

He ignored me. "I'd like to get a response from him before the story is live tonight. Any idea where I can find him?"

I sighed. "No idea."

"From what I hear, he's your dog sitter." He sauntered closer toward me. I retreated to behind the counter.

"Mine and a dozen others."

He pulled out his spiral notebook and flipped pages. He read his notes silently. "I heard his mother disappeared while hiking twenty years ago. He believes his stepfather killed her."

I folded my arms across my chest. "What does that have to do with me?"

"That's a strong motive for murder, don't you think?"

"You know, it was just yesterday you were convinced Grey pushed Mason down the stairs because of a bad business deal."

He held up a hand. "Hey, I wasn't the only one who thought he was guilty."

"Not us," Betty said. She stood next to me, chest out, shoulders back.

Mr. TV shot her a wary look. I didn't blame him. I'd worry she'd pat me down again, too.

"You've been spending a lot of time with Quinn Reed lately." He studied me. "She was Mason's mistress when he was married to Colin's mother. What's her relationship with Colin Sellers now? She has to have an opinion on Colin murdering her husband."

Darby hadn't mentioned that nugget of information. Had Colin honestly forgotten to tell her? Or was he still keeping secrets? "I've got nothing more to say. Your two minutes are up."

He looked like he wanted to say more. Betty handed me the phone and recited the number for the police station.

Recognizing defeat, MacAvoy showed decent judgment and tucked tail and ran.

"He has nice lips," Betty said.

I blinked. "What? Who?"

"That TV reporter. I was watching his lips while all those lies fell outta his mouth. That's when I noticed, he has kissable lips."

"I thought you were faithful."

"Faithful, Cookie. Not blind."

CHAPTER TWENTY

A couple of hours later I stood in the doorway of Evan Dodd's understated office, hoping his loose lips would drop helpful information about what Mason might have been hiding. The receptionist was out but had left a note on her desk for me to go through.

I found Evan behind a small metal desk, his long sleeves bunched up to his elbows. His brows were furrowed in concentration as he studied a spreadsheet on his computer, the pale light casting a blue glow to his face. If this didn't work, I wasn't sure how to get information out of the nervous bookkeeper.

I knocked on the open door. "Am I early?"

He jerked away from the screen and looked up. It took a second for his eyes to focus on me.

"Sorry, I didn't mean to startle you."

He minimized his screen then stood, waving me into his office. "No, no. I've been expecting you. Have a seat." He ran his hand through his dark unruly curls.

I sat in the orange vinyl chair across from him. Spreadsheets and graphs cluttered his desk. I searched for a photo of his girlfriend, but I didn't see one. "Thanks for seeing me on such short notice."

"My receptionist didn't say what you wanted to see me about. What can I do for you?" His wobbly voice broke. He cleared this throat.

"I'm concerned my accountant might be skimming off the top. I don't really know anyone else, so I thought you might be able to give me some advice on what to look for."

He removed his glasses to clean the lenses. "Who's your accountant?"

"I'd rather not say. You know, in case I'm wrong, I don't want to malign his character."

He slipped his glasses back in place. "Smart. Otherwise an unfounded allegation like that is a lawsuit waiting to happen."

"Exactly. I'm so glad you understand. Is there an easy way for me to tell if money is missing?"

"You should review your vendor accounts. Make sure you recognize who they are and what type of business you do with them. That's the easiest way to skim small amounts. Next, double check that your taxes have been paid. You can also make sure there are no outstanding loans you're not aware of. Your accountant could have taken out a loan in your business name, kept the money, and you end up paying for it."

I was spellbound. I had no idea how easy it was to take someone else's money. I hadn't planned on personally auditing my books when I walked into his office, but I was going to now.

"Thank you. You've been informative. Seriously. I had no idea."

He folded his fingers together and leaned in. "It's easy to trust the wrong person."

It was the opening I needed. "Is that what Mason did? Trust the wrong person?"

He blinked. "I'm sorry. I don't know what you mean."

"I've been thinking about the painting and Quinn's insistence that she audit her own books. At first, the only thing that made sense was that Mason was keeping money from Quinn."

"I'm sure you understand I can't confirm or deny that statement."

"Like I said, that's what I thought at first. Then I learned Mason didn't take the painting with him. He had it delivered here. Not to his home."

Evan swallowed. "That's true."

"According to Bree Young, his mistress, it's because he was planning on leaving Quinn. But then something happened, and Mason decided to return the painting. Only it wasn't the same one Grey had sold him. I believe Mason had no idea he was trying to pass off a copy as the original."

Evan's gaze darted around the room looking for a quick escape. Unfortunately for him, I was seated between him and the door.

"If the painting was here, the only way that exchange could have happened is through you."

He remained silent. But judging from the panic in his eyes, my supposition was right or awfully close. All those years of listening to Grey talk about white-collar crimes had paid off.

I pressed on. "Like you just explained, taking money in small amounts is easy to explain away. With someone like Mason, who had a bulging bank account, I'm guessing you've been skimming off the top for years."

"You need to leave."

I was just getting started. "But like all criminals who get away with their crimes, you got comfortable, greedy. You saw an opportunity to swap a three-hundred-thousand-dollar painting for a copy worth one-tenth of its true value. How'd you manage that? You'd have to know someone."

He must have realized his mouth was hanging open. He closed it with a snap.

"Am I close?" I asked.

"Well, this is embarrassing." He loosened the collar of his dress shirt. "I — I can explain. My girlfriend has a bad spending habit. I borrowed a few thousand to cover her debts last year. I paid it back the following month. No one was the wiser."

Ha! I was right. "That was the problem, wasn't it? You got away with it so you tried it again."

He reddened. "Maybe a few more times. Anything I may have borrowed, I've returned."

"Everything?"

"Almost everything," he admitted, his face a bright scarlet.

I assumed he was talking about the painting. "You know, my Grandma Tillie used to say, 'If you find yourself in a hole, the first thing to do is stop digging.' I can't offer you any better advice than that."

"If I'd have known Mason was going to change his mind and sell that wretched painting, I would have never switched them. But it was too late. I'd made the deal and couldn't back out. Black-market art is dangerous and not at all profitable. I only got ten percent of fair market value."

From what Grey had said, the only way to make money off stolen art work was to sit on it for years or trade it for other black-market items.

"Mason had to have been upset when he realized what you'd done."

His eyes widened. "He was livid. I've never seen him so angry. He threatened to turn me over to the police."

"So he attacked you, and in defending yourself you accidently pushed him down the stairs."

"What?" He jumped up. "I may be a thief, but I am not a murderer. You think I'd kill Mason for money?"

I scoffed. "People have killed for less. And from what you said, it sounds like you needed it. I'm sure you were terrified all your misdeeds were about to be found out if he called the police."

"Well, he must have changed his mind. The police have never questioned me about it. Besides, I wasn't the only one who needed Mason's money. Talk to his mistress, Bree Young."

"You knew about her?"

"Of course. Who do you think cut her

monthly checks?"

"Good point."

"The day before Mason was killed, he broke up with her and she wasn't happy about her free ride dumping her on the side of the road."

CHAPTER TWENTY-ONE

I called Grey and asked him to meet me so I could share my information about the bookkeeper and the painting. He suggested we meet at Main Beach. After circling the parking area, I finally found a spot. I slipped on my sunglasses and headed to the board-walk looking for Grey. I spotted him sitting on a bench near the sand volleyball pit. He looked relaxed in his jeans, t-shirt, and sunglasses. He noticed me at the same time and waved me over.

"Thanks for meeting me here. I was at the ARL when you called." He handed me a fresh fruit tart from the French restaurant behind us.

"You know, since we broke up, I've lost six pounds. I didn't realize you fed me so often."

A lazy smile pulled at his mouth. "I noticed."

I took a bite of the tart and closed my

eyes, savoring the flaky crust. "This is so good," I said around a mouthful of dessert.

"What were you doing at the ARL? Are you ready to foster again?" As long as I'd known Grey, he'd fostered hard-to-place large dogs. His availability was determined by the case he was working on. He was an excellent foster parent.

He nodded. "I let them know I'm available. There are a couple of guys I might be a good match for. A chocolate lab and a boxer."

I smiled. "You know I'm going to be partial to the boxer."

"I was sure you would be. So what did you find out?"

I licked custard off my fingers. "Like we suspected, Evan was embezzling. He swears he's paid back everything he's *borrowed,* except for the difference in the paintings."

"Do you believe him?"

I shook my head. "No. He said he had no idea Mason was going to try and sell the painting. Evan had switched it with the fake, and when Mason figured it out, he went ballistic. Threatened to turn him in. Evan thinks he changed his mind because the police never darkened his door."

Grey watched the ocean beat the sand. The sound of the crashing waves carried to where we sat, which I found relaxing. I waited for him to share whatever he was working out mentally.

"He reported the theft to the FBI," he finally said.

It took a minute to register everything that one sentence communicated.

"That's why he had your phone number. He must have just called you."

"I don't think he knew he'd be meeting Agent *Donovan.* I arrived at the store around nine thirty that morning. The door was locked. I knocked, but no one answered. I thought either we got the time mixed up or he had changed his mind. Damn. I was hoping that talking to him about the painting swap would lead to a break in the counterfeit purses case."

I sagged against the wooden bench. "Instead, he ended up dead and you a prime suspect. I don't understand. Weren't you taking a big chance on exposing your role with the FBI by meeting him?"

"We had a plan. If he cooperated with the FBI, we'd protect him."

"That's a big *if.* The minute you stepped in the store your cover was blown."

"Only if I immediately identified myself when I saw him. There was no need —" He stopped abruptly. "It doesn't matter now."

"I guess it doesn't."

We sat in silence again. In the old days, this was when I'd reach out and squeeze his hand. Tell him he was amazing and that the case would still be solved, even without Mason Reed.

"You should stop by the shop tomorrow morning, around ten," I said. "We're holding a small thank-you brunch for the Angels with Paws donors. If you wanted to flex your muscles, you can come by at six tonight and help set up tables."

He glanced in my direction. "You sure you want me there? People will talk."

I smiled. "Most of our murder suspects will be there. Let's hope they talk, and we can prove one way or the other if Colin murdered his stepfather or not."

It was almost seven o'clock. Grey, Betty, Agent James, and I rearranged merchandise to make room for four tall cocktail tables the catering company had delivered for the following morning's event.

"I didn't realize we'd have to destroy our shop for someone else's party," Betty complained, dropping a basket of tennis balls against the wall.

"No complaining. We have plenty of help."

Betty scoffed. "If you haven't noticed,

we've been ditched."

I did notice. At some point Grey had slipped outside with my new intern. I sure hoped Grey only shared information and wasn't attempting to gather it. I had a strong suspicion Agent James wouldn't hesitate to report Grey for involving himself in the investigation after he'd been told to stay out of it.

Betty and I put a black tablecloth over the last table. I looked around the shop, pleased with what we were able to accomplish in thirty minutes. We'd managed to strategically place the tables in areas of the room without the need to move displays and racks of merchandise. Even Betty's pawlish and treat jars were still in their ideal spot near the register, ready to be picked up for an impulse buy.

Grey burst through the front door with a broad smile and a bounce to his step. A bounce I hadn't seen in almost a year.

"What's with you all the sudden?" I returned his infectious smile.

He grabbed me by the waist and swung me around. "Whoa there, Cowboy." I laughed, gripping his broad shoulders.

"My turn, Handsome." Betty held out her arms waiting for her turn.

Grey set me down and pressed a quick

kiss on my mouth. "I'm back in the game," he whispered in my ear.

My heart leapt for joy. "I'm happy for you."

On instinct, I hugged him. I caught my breath as his strong arms wrapped tightly around me. It felt so right. But I couldn't think about it now. We had a party to plan and suspects to gather.

"Oh, someone's getting lucky tonight," Betty shouted.

Out of the corner of my eye I saw Agent James standing next to the coffee bar. I felt bad for him. The crestfallen look on his inexperienced face spoke volumes. Grey was back, but Agent James was out.

CHAPTER TWENTY-TWO

It was the morning of the open house, and I was feeling lucky. No, I didn't *get* lucky. I just had a feeling that good things were going to happen that day. Especially after Grey's big news the night before. I could feel we were close to solving Mason's murder.

Bow Wow Boutique was buzzing with goodwill and laughter. The caterers had provided a large spread of scrambled eggs, bacon, scones, and fresh fruit. The donors had made quick work devouring the breakfast food as they came and went. I even spied a handful of guests scoring a doggie bag to take with them when they left.

I'd set up the coffee bar and added iced tea as an option. A carafe of orange juice and champagne flutes had appeared out of nowhere. I silently thanked the caterers for their extra touch, and filled a glass.

All in all, about fifteen donors were in attendance. Not bad for a last-minute invitation. I was certain the good turnout was because they loved Ella Johns. She had a way of inspiring loyalty in others.

Ever the gracious hostess, Ella fluttered around the room in her lilac cold-shoulder dress, expressing her sincerest appreciation to each person for their support. She'd pulled her short auburn hair into a side-swept bob, perfectly framing her elegant face. Ella's surprise guest was her newest seizure response dog, Chip. The energetic Golden was the hit of the gathering.

Chip faithfully remained by her side, sharing his nutty lopsided grin, inviting attention as they worked the room. I smiled hearing Ella's hearty laughter boom across the room. I adored everything about Angels with Paws and was honored Ella had asked for my help.

I waved over Agent James, who the FBI had insisted remain on the case with Grey.

"How can I help, Ms. Langston?"

I glared at him. "Stop calling me that. Kids these days call their bosses by their first name."

"How can I help, Me-Melinda?" he stuttered.

He was a strange mix of innocence and brains. I grabbed his sleeve and dragged him through the room. I introduced him as my new intern and tried to steer the conversation to topics that might help him with the case. He seemed surprised, yet grateful.

Satisfied our guests had everything they needed, I refilled my juice glass. I stood back, sipping my drink, and took, what I like to call, "suspect attendance." Quinn, check. Leo, check. And a surprise guest of my own — Bree Young. Check. Her attendance today was a major coup. I'd asked Evan to contact her, requesting that she attend. I had a gut feeling that if she really did love Mason, she'd like to confront the evil wife.

Speaking of Quinn, she had arrived shortly after ten. Judging by her sour expression, this was the last place she wanted to be and was likely planning a hasty escape. In the words of my Grandma Tillie, "She was as warm as an ice cube."

Quinn had managed to avoid Leo, who was wrapped up in a lively conversation with Betty and Grey, but that didn't stop her from watching him with her eagle eye. I'd tasked Grey with keeping an eye on Leo. The more attention the sketchy fellow paid to Betty, the more he landed on my radar.

Although Darby had been invited as the official photographer, I wasn't expecting her to show. I'm sure some people use work to keep their mind off of their personal trouble. In Darby's case, being surrounded by possible suspects of the crime her new boyfriend was accused of committing wasn't about to her distract her from the current situation.

I realized Nina was missing. I had a bad feeling about her finances and wasn't convinced she'd come since she had promised she'd bring a new check. I decided to cover her donation anonymously if Evan wasn't able to get her money problems fixed. It wasn't going to break my bank, and it seemed like the right move.

Although our guests were already leaving, my suspects remained, but they hadn't interacted yet. It was time to intervene and make something happen. Betty and Grey were chatting alone near the display of pawlish and treat jars. Had Leo left and I'd missed it? I caught Grey's eye and silently asked about Leo with a questioning look. He pointed over my shoulder.

I turned to find Leo standing right behind me. I jumped back startled. How had he managed to corner me at the coffee bar and I not notice?

"Nice gathering. Thank you for the invite." He grabbed my hand and stuffed a folded piece of paper in it. "A little something to show my appreciation."

I recoiled, almost spilling my juice on his navy-blue sport coat. "I don't take bribes." The words fell out before I could stop them.

His bushy eyebrows furrowed. "It's a donation to the cause. Isn't that why you invited me?"

I felt my face warm. *Wow, jump to conclusions much, Mel?* I held the check toward him. "Sorry, I guess I'm a little distracted. You should give this to Ella. I'm sure she'd like to thank you personally."

"I'm sure it will mean just as much if you give it to her." He patted the front of his jacket as if looking for something.

I didn't have a pocket to stuff the paper inside so I clutched it in my fist. I was nosey, and I wanted to see how much the check was for without his watching me. If the amount was substantial, which I had a feeling it was, I wanted Ella to have the opportunity to thank Leo. That's what she would want.

"I'll go give this to her." I turned on my heel to leave.

His laid his warm hand on my shoulder. I froze.

"Melinda, don't go. I'd like to make you an offer you can't refuse."

I faced him slowly. Suddenly, he was a wise guy. What was he going to do next? Pull out a gun and tell me to say hello to his *other* little friend?

My guard firmly in place, I waited to hear his irresistible offer.

"I'd like to buy your shop. I'll give you top dollar. Name your price." He held his checkbook in one hand, a ballpoint pen in the other.

I choked on a laugh. He paused while I composed myself. I expected him to brush it off, claim it was all a joke. But he didn't. And he wasn't smiling. He was dead serious.

I was offended that he thought he could buy me off so easily. "Bow Wow isn't for sale."

"Now, don't be hasty. Think about it before you dismiss my offer out of hand."

I shrugged off his patronizing tone. "I don't need the money. I like what I do. Why do you want it anyway? I thought you were in to import-export services, not a pampered pet boutique?"

"For my Betty girl, of course." His practiced smile didn't reach his eyes. He was lying.

Why would he want to give such an expensive and time-consuming gift to a woman he'd just met? As much as Betty might pretend she was running the place, I knew she had no real desire to do so. She liked the freedom to come and go as she pleased, making a little cash on the side.

"Did she tell you she wanted you to buy the shop for her?" I asked.

"No. it's a surprise."

It dawned on me that he probably wanted to run his import-export business through here. Could he be behind the counterfeit purse ring? I tilted my head, studying him. What was it Quinn had said, something about the 'word of a dead man'?

"Did you offer to purchase Quinn's shop too? Is that what you two were talking about when I interrupted you?"

His charm vanished. "Mason and I had a verbal understanding, which Quinny backed out of. We were working on the purchase agreement the day before his untimely death. She'll come back around."

Yeah, yeah. After she finds a horse head in her bed. He shouldn't hold his breath.

Betty's bright floral orange muumuu caught my eye. She pushed around Leo and yanked my arm.

"Cat fight near the doggie bridal gowns," she snickered. "Let's go."

I rushed after Betty, secretly excited. Two

of my suspects had finally collided.

Grey stood between Bree and Quinn who had faced off in front of the handmade doggie bridal gowns, just like Betty had said.

"You need to leave," Quinn demanded, her face deathly calm.

Yikes. I was concerned for Bree. She may be tall and appear strong, but Quinn looked like it was a short trip to crazy town, and she had room for one more — preferably an Amazon Barbie.

"I have every right to be here. I was personally invited." Bree straightened to her full, unnatural height, standing a good five inches over Quinn, who was wearing flats again.

Quinn's face remained eerily composed. "You're a home wrecker and a leech."

Bree arched a blond eyebrow. "You would know. Mason said you two were lovers when he was married to his first wife."

A loud gasp rolled through the shop. Ouch. That accusation supported what Colin had told Darby.

"Now, girls, stop your arguing," Betty piped up. "You're both pretty." She nudged Grey. "Do something before they destroy our shop."

"No." I grabbed his arm. "Let them talk."

I pulled Betty next to me. Even though I

wanted to hear what they had to say, I'd witnessed enough bickering women to know it was possible the name calling and allegations could turn into hair pulling and yelling. The smart move was to stay out of arm's reach.

Quinn's eyes darted around the room, realizing a handful of guests were still hanging around, their attention now focused on her and Bree.

Bree must have taken Quinn's silence as a sign of weakness and went in for the kill. "You know Mason was leaving you, right? He sold the store. We were going to live in Italy."

Quinn scoffed. "You're so stupid. He was never going to leave me. I know where the skeletons are buried. In the end, Mason only cared about himself."

Interesting choice of words, "skeletons are buried." Was she referring to Colin or something else?

Bree sucked in a shocked breath. "That's a lie. He had it all planned out. He was going to sell his painting, and we'd use that money to escape from you."

Quinn's evil laugh made me shudder. "That was a fake. Evan sold the real one weeks ago. There's no money. Mason fooled you."

Bree was about to say something when the front door opened. There stood Darby and Colin. This time I gasped. Wide-eyed, I looked at Grey. He shook his head. My instinct was to protect Darby, but Grey was right, we needed to let this play out. Or he was possibly trying to keep me out of the line of fire.

Quinn stumbled back when she saw Colin. "It *is* you," she cried softly.

He swung in Quinn's direction. A lock of blond hair fell across forehead. Darby grabbed his hand and muttered something.

"I guess someone made bail," Betty muttered.

"He was never arrested," I corrected her for Darby's benefit.

Bree pointed her finger at Colin. "That's the man I saw leaving the store the morning Mason died," she announced to the room. A little too loudly. A little too dramatically.

Grey quietly moved to stand between all parties. I noticed Agent James stood on the opposite side of the room from Grey, his gaze darting around, assessing the situation. I was awed at how quickly he'd had Grey's back.

It was the most inopportune time for a life-changing realization, but I'd had one anyway. Yes, Grey couldn't tell me details of his undercover work, or how dangerous a case might be, but it shouldn't have mattered. He was never alone. Someone had faithfully had his back. I'd been selfish to believe his sidekick had to have always been me. That was a lot to digest.

I returned my focus to what Grey was asking Bree. "What were you doing at the store?"

She blinked. "I was there to meet Mason." She must have realized where this conversation was headed. "He was dead when I got there," she added quickly.

Colin stepped forward, Darby remaining at his side. "He was already dead when I got there, too," he stated simply.

Quinn shook her head. "Why come here? Why now?"

"You know why. Did you do it? Did you kill Mason? Did you help him kill my mother?" With each question, he'd taken one more step closer to Quinn.

Grey never took his eyes off the confrontation unfolding before us. He shifted closer toward Quinn, ready to act if needed.

She shook her head. "No. It was her." She pointed a finger at Bree. Her accusation settled into an unexpectant silence.

Bree's eyes darkened. "He was going to leave you, but you murdered him first."

Okay, this was about to get out of hand. I glanced around the room at the embarrassed interest on everyone's face. I had to admit, it was difficult to ignore a train wreck when it happened right in front of you. Time to pull the plug on our live soap opera reenactment.

I took one step forward. "Okay, everyone let's take a break."

No one moved. I looked to Grey for help. He shot me an oh-now-you-want-my-help look? Yes, I did.

"Quinn, you look like you could use some fresh air." Grey took her by the elbow and led her outside.

And with that, the show was over. Don't get me wrong, there was a loud murmur of gossip bouncing around the room, but the possibility of a Laguna Beach Real Housewives orange-juice-throwing fight, had been extinguished. Quinn had said something important that I wanted to talk to Grey about, but I couldn't remember what it was. I had gotten sidetracked by Darby and Colin's unexpected entrance. I'd have to ask Grey later if he'd caught it.

I turned to Betty to ask her to help me begin the cleanup. I caught her scribbling in her notebook. "What are you doing," I asked in a hushed voice.

"Taking notes. I think Amazon Barbie did it. She was already bent over his body when I showed up."

"But Malone cleared her," I argued.

Although, I was just assuming that was the case. All he'd ever said was that he'd talked to her. Had I been barking up the wrong tree?

Within fifteen minutes, the shop was empty and the four of us began cleaning up. Darby had offered to stay and help. I loved her generous spirit and loyalty. I sent her home and asked if she and Colin would stop by to check on Missy. After the day's performance, I'd changed my opinion on Colin Sellers.

Grey and Agent James broke down the tables and helped load them on the catering truck parked behind the building. I found Betty peeking out the front door.

"What are you doing?" I came up behind her and looked over her shoulder.

Leo and Quinn faced each other, obviously arguing.

"How long have they been there?" I asked.

"Since your handsome man left her at the curb."

I'd never noticed how toned Quinn's arms were until she was waving them angrily in the air. She was close enough to pop Leo on the nose if she wasn't careful.

I wondered if I should tell Betty about Leo's offer. I didn't like the guy, and I didn't want her spending any more time with him. But Betty was a stubborn gal, and the minute I told her not do something, she'd jump in feet first just to prove me wrong.

Quinn folded her arms across her chest as Leo talked. "Look at how they're standing so close together. They look like lovers more than adversaries."

"He's a complicated guy, Cookie." She sighed like an infatuated teenager.

I rested my hand gently on her shoulder. "That's not necessarily good."

She pressed against the window. "Shh. I'm trying to hear what they're saying."

I rolled my eyes. "Why not just go outside?"

We watched Quinn poke her finger into Leo's chest.

"Did you know he's trying to take her store away from her?" I asked.

"He told me they had an agreement."

"I think his agreement was with Mason. I don't believe she knew about it."

"I bet that's what they're arguing about."

Leo said something that made Quinn yell

obscenities loud and clear. She shoved him so hard he stumbled.

Betty whistled. "Quinn's one tough broad."

Yes, she was.

CHAPTER TWENTY-THREE

I was pulled out of a deep, dreamless sleep by an unexpected phone call at an ungodly hour the next morning.

"Hello," I croaked.

"Melinda Langston?" asked the male voice on the other end.

I sat up slowly. I recognized the voice, but I couldn't yet place it. "Yes."

"This is Officer Hostas. I'm calling to inform you that your business was broken into this morning."

My heart jumped. "Bash 'n Dash?"

"It looks that way."

I tossed aside the covers and hopped out of bed, wide awake. Angry tears burned the back of my eyes. How dare some bloody criminal trash my business?

"I'm on my way."

I immediately decided not to inform Betty until after I had a look. It wouldn't matter what I told her; she'd show up and make a scene. I threw on a pair of worn jeans and my graphic tee with the saying, "Sit happens." It seemed appropriate. Not sure what type of damage I'd find when I got to the boutique, I shoved my size nines inside an old pair of work boots and pulled on a hoodie.

I revved up the Jeep and raced to Bow Wow. As I rolled to a stop in front the shop, I caught my breath. Three police cars and a shattered front window greeted me. The police had the front of the shop blocked off with orange cones. I had to drive an additional block to find a place to park.

I released my breath and slid out of the Jeep. The slam of the door echoed in my head. What if someone had been at the store when it was broken into?

Officer Hostas met me outside the store. "Sorry, Mel."

"Look on the bright side. We're not meeting over a dead body," I joked weakly.

He nodded in agreement. "This is a new one for us."

I took a deep breath and focused my anger at whoever was responsible. "Let's take a look around and see what's been taken. If the last three break-ins are an indicator, I'm guessing nothing."

Hostas looked over my shoulder. "I'll meet

you inside."

I turned around to see what had caught his attention. None other than Mr. TV himself. Lately he'd become a regular nuisance in my life.

The Channel 5 News van slowed in front of the shop, looking for a place to pull over. A uniformed police officer ordered the van to move on. MacAvoy caught sight of me and motioned that he wanted to come in. I shook my head, then spun around and stomped through shattered glass.

Two uniformed officers stood inside the boutique waiting for me. They asked a few general questions as I looked around.

By the time Hostas had returned, I'd been able to quickly survey the property.

"Don't worry about the reporter. We'll keep him out." Hostas rested his beefy hands on his duty belt.

"Thank you. I have to admit, it's a little unsettling having you on my side for once."

"Let's hope we don't get used to it. Other than the front door and large picture window being smashed, it doesn't look like much has been disturbed. It follows suit with the other break-ins."

The safe was untouched, the register was untouched. Not that there was much to take; I'd made a bank run last night before

I went home.

"What do you think?" Hostas asked.

I shook my head. "I'm confused. Why break in and not take anything? Other than Betty's vase of flowers knocked onto the floor, nothing else seemed to be disturbed. It doesn't make any sense."

"We're working on a few leads. Do you have a working surveillance camera?"

I shook my head. "I meant to get one, but I kept putting it off. What about the other break-ins? Did they have cameras?"

"A couple."

"And," I prompted.

"Not helpful."

I sighed. "When do you think I can open for business?"

"We should be out of your way soon." He looked out front. "Here comes trouble."

Suddenly, Betty and Grey burst on the scene. I wondered which one Hostas considered trouble.

Betty, in a hot-pink jogging suit, her straw handbag swinging from the crook of her elbow, raced toward me. "Cookie, are you okay?"

She lunged for me, hugging me tight as soon as she made contact.

I patted her back. "I'm fine."

She let go of me and surveyed the shop.

She shook her head in denial.

I looked at Grey. "From what I can tell, the boutique is fine. Nothing's been disturbed. Nothing taken. Just a bashed-in front window and door. How did you know about it?"

"It's on the news," Grey said softly.

"Look what they did to our little shop." Betty found her favorite products. Assured they weren't damaged, she opened her purse. "Don't you worry, Cookie. I'm on the case."

"No you're not. This is police business."

Betty ignored me. She sidled up to Officer Hostas. "You're dusting for fingerprints, right?"

He grunted. Taking that as a yes, Betty moved on.

"What time did you leave last night, Cookie?" She pulled the notebook out of her handbag.

I sighed. "The same time as you. We all left together."

"That's right." She scribbled a few notes on the paper.

Grey gingerly pulled the spiral pad from her hands and tucked it in his back pocket. "Come with me."

"This isn't a good time, Handsome. Cookie and I need to figure out who's

316

behind the Smash and Dashes. I'll take my notebook back now."

I shook my head; she couldn't even get the name right.

"No, you don't. Once the police have finished their part, we need to help Mel clean up. We need to get the shop open as soon as possible. People need to know we're open for business."

Betty had been so caught up in solving the Bash 'n Dash, she hadn't noticed her flowers were no longer on the counter. "Where are my flowers?" She ran to where her flowers laid strewn on the floor by the wall.

"They knocked over my flowers." Betty gingerly gathered her beat-up flowers by their broken stems. "This was unnecessary. Why?" She sounded like she was about to cry.

Grey bent over to help. "Be careful of the glass."

"You just wait until I get my hands on whoever did this," Betty said.

"Don't move," Grey barked out.

Everyone froze. He called over Officer Hostas and pointed to something on the ground. Hostas pulled a latex glove from his back pocket and tugged it on. He picked up whatever it was he and Grey were studying to take a closer look.

"You're right. I'll bag it," Hostas said.

Betty and I pushed our way over to Grey. "What did you find?" I asked.

"A bug."

Betty let out a disgruntled, "Humph." She kicked a piece of debris aside. "Why is he going to bag an insect as evidence?"

"Not that type of bug. A listening device. Someone was eavesdropping on Bow Wow."

CHAPTER TWENTY-FOUR

A large crowd had gathered on the sidewalk in front of Darby's studio, mostly loyal customers concerned for Betty's and my safety. The overwhelming show of support moved me to tears. I jokingly tried to guilt them all into buying the last of the dog sweaters. They didn't feel that bad.

Darby had texted, checking on us and asked if we needed anything. I reassured her we were fine and promised to call that afternoon. I even had a voicemail from my sassy cousin, Caro. She'd seen the report and wanted to make sure we were okay. I swallowed past the lump in my throat. It was moments like this when you missed your family.

I'd given Betty the day off. She rambled on about timing and graduation. I had asked her to explain, but she'd clammed up. I had a strong suspicion whatever she was talking about had to do with her one-thirty appointments. And an even stronger suspicion it had to do with a private investigator's license.

"Grey, go home." We stood on the sidewalk across the street from the boutique.

"No." His one word packed a wealth of emotion.

I could hear the faint sound of birds chirping over my steady pulse beating in my ears. A slight breeze rustled the leaves in the trees we waited under. Judging by the weather it should have been a calm, relaxing day. Life had other plans.

I stared at the clean-up crew Grey had managed to find in less than two hours. They moved quickly, cleaning up the broken glass, and had already covered the front door with plywood.

At last we were alone and I could ask the one question that had been begging to be answered. "Please tell me that was an FBI-issued listing device."

"It's not."

I'd been afraid that's what he was going to say.

My hands shook as I pushed up the sleeves of my hoodie. Adrenaline, I reassured myself. "I'm fine. I promise."

His sharp blue eyes focused on the men across the street as if willing them to work faster. "The crew will be finished by the afternoon. I've called a window company to take measurements and replace the broken glass. They've assured me you'll be back in business by tomorrow."

Conflicting emotion clogged my throat. I couldn't speak. I nodded my thanks.

After a few minutes I finally found my voice. "I need to have a cry and release all my pent-up emotions, but I can't with you standing here."

He nodded. He gently placed a hand at the small of my back. "I'll walk you to the Jeep."

I sighed, facing him. "I'm not going to break. I just need to let go of . . ." I motioned with my hand, hoping he understood what I was struggling to put into words.

"This isn't only about you."

The air stilled around us. He reached out and gently caressed my cheek. "Don't worry about the shop. I've got it under control. Call your family and tell them you're on your way."

I shook my head. "No. I will not run. No one was hurt. Bow Wow will open at eleven o'clock on the dot tomorrow morning."

CHAPTER TWENTY-FIVE

I'd made it halfway home when I realized it was obvious who was behind the listening device. I had to believe Grey had already figured it out, which would explain his stoic demeanor. If it wasn't the FBI, that left only one person. Leo Montana, the man who had bestowed the flowers to Betty in first place. How could I have missed that?

Now that I knew, I wanted to talk to the person who seemed to understand him best — Quinn Reed. I hung a tight U-turn and aimed the Jeep to Hot Handbags. I parked a few stores down from my destination, not wanting to alert Quinn of my arrival in case she was looking out her window.

I entered the store determined to learn the truth about Leo and why he wanted to buy Quinn's boutique so badly. And why Bow Wow had caught his interest.

An offer I couldn't refuse? Really?

Imagine my surprise when the first person

I saw was Betty Foxx standing in front of the sales counter of Hot Handbags.

"Cookie, what are you doing here?" She looked like she'd been caught with her hand in the treat jar.

I narrowed my eyes. An interesting turn of events. "What are *you* doing here?"

"Just catching up, right, Quinn, Old Buddy?" Betty shuffled away from me.

It didn't look like she and Quinn were chatting. It was just the three of us in the store. The perfect opportunity to question.

Quinn pressed her lips together. "Your *associate* thinks I had something to do with the break-in this morning."

Betty huffed. "I don't like the way you said 'associate.'"

I walked toward them slowly. Betty had obviously been giving Quinn the third degree, and now Quinn was on edge.

"I don't think you did, but I do think you know who is behind them." I continued moving toward them.

She shifted her weight, keeping the counter between us. "I don't know what you're talking about." Her uptight face didn't match her indifferent tone.

"Leo offered me a blank check to buy Bow Wow. Why?"

"Ask him." Defiance dripped from her words.

"I'm asking you," I said. "He made it clear to me he also wants your shop."

"You're not selling, right, Cookie?" Betty's distress at the possibility of my selling the shop only confirmed my suspicions about Leo.

I shook my head. "Never. The shop is ours." I faced Quinn and locked on to her irritated green eyes. "Quinn, why does Leo want to get his hands on our businesses? He's behind the break-ins, isn't he?"

Betty rubbed her hands together. "Oh! Cookie is on a quest." She pulled out the notebook Grey had returned to her on the condition she not investigate the Bash 'n Dash. "I overheard Leo on the phone. He thought I was in the bathroom, but I was snooping in his bedroom." She flipped pages. "He likes Chinese food, hair is fake. That's not it," she mumbled. "It's in here somewhere." She flipped through more pages.

Good lord, I did not want to know why she was nosing around in his bedroom. Thankfully, she bypassed that intimate detail as she read from her notes.

"Ah, here it is. He's running multiple illegal operations, including counterfeit phones, purses, and wine. He wants to use Hot Handbags as a cover. Plan B is to take over Bow Wow Boutique and turn it into a tourist shop." She flipped the notebook closed with satisfied grin.

I smiled like a proud parent on graduation day. "Nice work, Betty."

"He didn't have me fooled for a second. At least not once I learned he wore a rug," she scoffed.

"Hmmm." I didn't try to follow her logic. "Do you know who Leo was talking to?"

Betty narrowed her eyes in Quinn's direction. "That's why I'm here. I've graduated with honors from my PI class. I've got skills," she boasted. "I've started my own investigation, and I think it was her." She pointed at Quinn.

"Well, it wasn't." Quinn pressed against the counter. "Now that you know about Leo's side adventure in crime, you can leave. I suggest you go straight to the police. I have nothing to say."

I wasn't ready to depart just yet. I had more questions. A lot more. "Did Leo kill Mason?"

"If Colin didn't kill Mason, it must have been Leo. He pretends they were great friends, but the truth is, Leo hated Mason. Leo was always trying to convince me to leave Mason."

Betty shook her head. "Nope. Not buying it, Sister. Leo told me he keeps his friends close and his enemies closer. If that's true, Leo wouldn't kill him."

"Leo's connections were counting on him to close the deal with Mason. If Mason had changed his mind, Leo had bigger problems," Quinn said evenly.

I worked though Quinn's implications toward Leo. And her earlier comment about the word of a dead man. I had a bad feeling she was throwing Leo under the bus to protect herself.

"If he killed Mason, he'd lose the store. They only had a 'gentleman's agreement.' And from what you and Evan have said, it sounds like Leo had spent too much time priming Mason to sell. Leo unequivocally thought he was getting the store."

"Who's Evan?" Betty asked.

"Their bookkeeper," I explained. At the mention of Evan's name, I remembered there was something Quinn had said that bothered me. I just couldn't put my finger on it.

Quinn refused to comment.

I tried a different angle. "Leo bugged my shop. Do you know why?"

Quinn sighed in annoyance. "Why do you

think? You had what he wanted."

Bow Wow. "Because I refused to sell to him? He thought he could blackmail me into selling?"

She shrugged. "I wouldn't put it past him. If he couldn't find someone's Achilles heel, he'd have his crew break in. Most of the time customers were scared off. Businesses that were cash poor were looking for a quick sell."

"And Leo would come to the rescue. Swoop in and offer to buy them out. Probably dirt cheap." Only in my case it had strengthened my resolve. Exactly how dangerous was Leo?

Betty frowned. "The scoundrel."

"It was working," Quinn said simply.

"Until someone pushed Mason down the stairs," I said.

A glint of evil flashed in her eyes just long enough for me to catch it. A shiver of fear ran down my spine. Maybe it was time to leave. Quinn knew an awful lot about Leo's dealings to be completely innocent. Betty and I needed to get out and head straight for the police station and talk to Malone.

I grabbed Betty's arm. "Let's go. We have enough to hand over to the police."

I could see the change of plans on Quinn's face. In a split second she realized that she'd cleared Leo. And implicated herself.

And I realized the same. Holy crapola.

Quinn pulled out what looked like a toy gun and pointed it at us. "Now that you've put it all together, you didn't think I'd let you just waltz out of here, did you?"

Well, yes, I did.

I swallowed hard. "Where'd you get the gun?"

"It's Mason's. Never left home without it."

My stomach tightened in fear. I slowly raised my hands showing I wasn't armed. "This is a bad idea. You don't want to do this. As it stands you can still claim Mason's fall was an accident. If you shoot us, that's murder, no getting around it."

"Only if they catch me," she spat out. "I've gotten away with it before."

Betty glared at Quinn. "The Dog Whisperer was right. You did kill his mom."

She shrugged. "Mason pushed her off a cliff while they were hiking."

How fitting that he was pushed to his death. Nothing as grand as a cliff, just a staircase. Karma was a pain.

"The skeletons you mentioned to Bree," I said.

"And they would have stayed that way if you two hadn't kept sticking your nose into my business."

My stomach dropped. What was that saying? "Curiosity killed the cat"? Yeah, it looked like that applied to Betty and me too.

My thoughts immediately turned to Grey. Just as we were reconnecting, I was about to die in a handbag store. I guess there were worse places to be murdered. Fear gripped my chest so tightly I thought I was having a heart attack. That fear was an incredible motivator.

"You made it my business when Grey was accused," I said.

I could hear Grey's voice in the back of my mind telling me to stop talking. But if she was spilling her guts to us, she had no intention of letting us walk out the door alive. Betty and I needed to save ourselves. The longer we kept her talking, the more time I had to formulate a plan.

"That was Mason's fault. He was ruining everything, carrying on about the painting like that."

"You never really know someone until you marry them," Betty said.

"You're not helping," I muttered.

Quinn waved her gun. "So true. Mason wasn't happy with what we had; he always needed more. More money, more women. I was over it. I had my own plans. And then he tried to sell that damn painting. Why couldn't he leave it alone? Evan and I had it all worked out."

I sucked in a deep breath. Well, shoot. That was it. I'd read everything wrong. It wasn't Leo and Quinn. It was Evan and Quinn. Evan's girlfriend was Quinn. They were planning on running away together. Quinn said Evan had sold the original painting weeks before Mason had tried to sell it himself.

Good grief. That explained an awful lot.

"If my man was cheating on me, I'd give him a knee strike right between the legs." Betty demonstrated, including a loud, "Ha!"

That was it. I could have kissed her. We just had to get close enough to Quinn. "Betty has taken self-defense. She's pretty good."

"Great. Granny has a hobby. It's time to go, Ladies."

No, no, no. We were not leaving the store. If we did, there was no telling where she'd take us.

"If you kill us, how will you explain our murders to Malone? He'll know we were here. He'll see our cars."

"Uh, Cookie, I walked."

Quinn, unimpressed with our comedy

routine, waved her gun toward the backdoor. "Get moving."

I dropped my hands. "No. If you're going to shoot us, do it here," I challenged her.

She looked at me like I'd lost my mind. Maybe I had.

Quinn reached across the counter and grabbed Betty's sleeve. "I said, we're leaving. I can't shoot you here. That would ruin my purses."

"Insurance doesn't cover that." Betty winked at me.

Betty yanked her arm from Quinn just enough to cause Quinn to lurch in to the counter. With a loud shout, Betty jumped up and shoved the heel of her palm directly to Quinn's nose.

Quinn doubled over as she yelled out in pain, dropping the gun on the counter. I grabbed it and backed away, pointing the gun at Quinn.

I sent a shaky smile in Betty's direction. "Nice work. Call 911."

She cradled her hand against her chest. "Why can't I hold the gun and you call 911?"

"FBI. Drop your weapon." Agent James suddenly burst through the backdoor.

Betty's eyes widened as FBI Agent Tom James stood in the hallway pointing his firearm at me, before aiming it at Quinn.

"Never mind. You can have the gun," Betty said.

Quinn's face was comical as she tried to process that my intern was really an FBI agent.

I laid the gun on the floor and kicked it toward Agent James. He cocked a questioning eyebrow.

I shrugged. "This isn't our first rodeo." Regardless of my offhanded comment, my heart was still racing from being held at gunpoint.

"Have you been following me? Do you give private lessons? I'm pretty sure I'll need to follow someone soon." Betty's excitement at possibly being followed obviously confused James.

"We've had this store under surveillance since Mason's murder. I got a call there was possible trouble."

"A real-life G-man." Betty's reverent tone almost made me giggle. Or the giggle may have been shock.

She elbowed me in the side. "I knew he wasn't an intern. I've got great intuition."

I pulled her into a brief hug. "Like you said, you are a star pupil."

CHAPTER TWENTY-SIX

"Cookie, I'm proud of you."

I smiled. "I didn't do it by myself. You and Grey helped."

She scoffed. "I'm not talking about that no-good Quinn Reed. I said from day one it was her, but no one believed me."

It was true. She did say it was the wife. Of course, she always says it's the spouse. At some point she had to be right. Turned out Quinn knew her husband's secret — that he was responsible for his first wife's death. She'd protected his secret until he could no longer give her what she wanted — money and status.

Darby and Colin were still dating. Now that all the facts had come to light, I didn't feel as suspicious of Colin. Turns out he had good reason to hate Mason and Quinn. He decided to stay in town and expand his dog sitting business. I had a feeling he'd have to turn down clients soon.

As for Betty, well she really had been sneaking off to PI classes. And acting classes. And firearm training. She was dead set on obtaining a PI license. She just needed someone to mentor her. Lord help us all if she ever found that person.

"Then what are you talking about?" I asked my trusty assistant.

She pulled out a white handkerchief with bluebells cross-stitched in the corner. Very gently she pulled back all the soft material revealing my Grandma Tillie's pin.

"Is it still in one piece?" I asked, reaching for the pin.

"Don't get sassy with me." She held out the handkerchief. "I think you're ready for it now."

I wanted to argue with her, but she was right.

She had no idea how right.

CHAPTER TWENTY-SEVEN

"We make a good team." Grey leaned back in the patio chair.

I grinned, batting my eyes. "I've always known we made a great team. It's much easier to help you, and stay out of your way, when I know what's going on."

His face turned serious. "Thanks for everything you did for me. For the case."

"I'll always have your back." My face grew warm as Grey studied me intently.

My stomach growled. I flipped open the pizza box. "We haven't had Gina's in ages."

He'd suggested we grab pizza and take it back to his place and watch the sun set on his back patio. It wasn't a hard sell. I pulled a slice from the box and dropped it on my paper plate. I was trying to keep my emotions in check, but it was difficult when Grey looked at me like I was more important than his favorite pizza.

"We've had a lot of good times here,"

Grey said.

"We have," I agreed easily. "You haven't touched the pizza yet."

His smiled softened his handsome face. "I'm enjoying watching you. I guess I forgot how much you love pizza."

"So what happens next with the undercover case?"

"Paperwork. Agent James is ready to escape Betty."

"I don't blame him. He deserves a medal for dealing with her. I can't believe he actually taught her how to tail someone. Although, she is the one who helped him nab Leo and take down the counterfeit purse ring. Not bad for his first case."

Grey chuckled. "I can't believe she was dating a mobster. What am I saying? Yes I can."

I swallowed more pizza. "I thought Malone was going to lock himself in jail at one point when we were explaining what went down at Hot Handbags."

"He needs a vacation."

That was the opening I needed. "Speaking of vacations. I was thinking we should catch a flight to Vegas tomorrow, stop by the wedding chapel, and finally get married."

"Is that the one with the Elvis impersonator?" Grey asked.

"No. The one with the drive-thru."

He took a long drink of water. "Is this a marriage proposal?"

"No. It's an elopement proposal. It's time to act."

"It's been an emotional few weeks. A lot has happened." He offered a way out. He obviously thought this was an impulsive proposal.

"I know what I'm saying, and I know what I feel. I love you. You love me. Let's stop planning for the future and start living. If you don't feel the same —"

"I was ready to marry you the very day I proposed the first time."

"But not the last two times?" I joked past the sudden lump in my throat.

"Every time. I'm just waiting for you."

The old Mel would have taken that as a slight. But I knew exactly what he was saying. "I'm ready."

"Okay. Are you serious about Vegas? It'll upset your mother."

I shook my head. "This isn't about her. Here's an idea. We'll go to Dallas this weekend as planned. She'll forgive me once I ask her to throw us the biggest wedding reception party Texas has ever seen. She'll forget all about the ceremony."

"Deal. There's one more thing," he said.
"Whatever you say."

CHAPTER TWENTY-EIGHT

The spur-of-the-moment wedding was as crazy as our courtship. Elvis did make a brief appearance, and after hearing about our journey to the altar, promptly burst out singing, "It's Now or Never." Appropriate. Grey was as sexy as always in his dark-charcoal Tom Ford suit. I had made a quick trip to Fashion Island in Newport the morning before we flew to Vegas. I found the perfect strapless wedding gown. A simple silk charmeuse, column gown that was so buttery smooth it felt like I was wearing a slip.

After the ceremony we took a helicopter ride over the Grand Canyon and made plans to come back and hike from the rim to the river for our first-year anniversary. The day was everything I had ever dreamed.

As much as I hated to return to Laguna, I had made a promise to Grey, and it was time to make good on it. I left him and

Missy at my place grabbing the last of Missy's belongings. We had decided to live at Grey's. More room for Missy, my shoes, and purses. As a wedding gift, he promised to build me a handbag and shoe closet. He knew the way to my heart.

I pulled up to Caro's house early in the morning, the quiet neighborhood similar to mine. Or should I say my old neighborhood? I touched my simple gold wedding band just to remind myself we'd actually gotten married.

I'd practiced my apology tour speech numerous times; starting with the announcement of our wedding, offering a sincere apology for being stubborn, and ending with a peace offering. I marched up the front walk to her door. I inhaled deeply, then exhaled. I practiced once more before I rang the bell.

"I'm sorry for hurting your feelings when I badmouthed your lousy ex-husband." I sighed. "I'm sorry for sticking my nose into your business." I nodded. That was better. "Caro, I'm sorry." I liked that one the best. Simple and to the point. She could fill in the blanks.

I gently slipped my hand inside my tote bag and wrapped my fingers around Grandma Tillie's brooch. I was doing the right thing . . . right? I shook off the doubts and pushed the doorbell. Dogbert barked once. I imagined Thelma and Louise swishing tails, wrapping around Caro's legs as she walked toward the door.

The door slowly opened.

"Hey, Caro. Guess what? I got —" I stopped midsentence.

I blinked. I couldn't be seeing what I thought I was seeing.

"Please tell me you're not real," I pleaded.

"Well, Melinda Sue Langston. My word, I'm surprised to see you here. I thought you and Caro weren't speaking." Mama Kat, Caro's mama, stood ramrod straight in front of me. Primed to put me in my place. Well, Hell's Bells. I released the brooch. That certainly put a damper on my plans.

I arched my eyebrow. "Does Caro know you're in her house?"

Kat huffed. "You're still unfunny. Caro's not here. She had a house call."

Oh, I'm sure she did. Caro was probably on her way out of town.

Caro's mama narrowed her cold, judgmental eyes. "Do you have a message for her?"

I thought about it for a minute.

"Tell her Mrs. Donovan has something for her. If she'd like to know what it is, she can meet her at Cress Street Beach at sunset."

"Who's Mrs. Donovan?" Mama Kat called from behind me.

"She'll know."

MISSY'S TAIL-WAGGING DRIED APPLE TREATS

Ingredients

2 Fuji or Honeycrisp apples

Directions

Preheat oven to 300°F.
Wash and dry 2 apples.
Remove core and seeds.
Slice apples into thin slices.
Place the apple slices on a sheet of parchment paper on a baking sheet.
Bake for 30 minutes.
Flip slices and bake for an additional 30 minutes or until slices feel dry.

Remove from oven, let them cool completely, and then store them in an airtight container with the rest of your pup treats. The slices can be kept in the refrigerator for one week.

MEL'S MEDITERRANEAN GRILLED CHEESE SANDWICH

Ingredients

2 tsp. butter
2 slices bread (Mel likes sourdough)
2 thin slices Roma tomato
1/4 cup spinach
2 Tbsp. pitted Kalamata olives
1 Tbsp. feta cheese
2 oz. fresh mozzarella slices

Directions

Spray a Foreman grill or sandwich press with cooking oil spray.

Preheat grill/sandwich press.

Spread butter evenly on both sides of each piece bread.

Top one slice of bread with tomato, spinach, olives, feta, mozzarella, and the second slice of bread.

Grill until bread is golden brown and cheese has melted.

ACKNOWLEDGEMENTS

First, thank you to the amazing team at Bell Bridge Books. Your continued support and belief in us for the past seven years is deeply appreciated. To our fabulous editor, Deb Dixon, you make us look good. Thank you for continuing to share your expertise. You made our dreams come true!

Christine Wittholm, our agent at Book Cents Literary Agency, thank you for your direction, advice and support.

Tami, Christine, and Cindy — endless gratitude for being on call, and for your support and belief in us. You are not only amazing critique partners, but lifetime friends. We love you.

A special thanks to Steve, Rachel, Seth, Josh, Sarah, Jeremy, and Colleen for all the meals you cooked, Starbucks you delivered, and times you cleaned the kitchen. Colleen, you give the best hugs!

To Chewy who crossed the Rainbow Bridge during the writing of *The Dogfather*. You were the best little buddy an animal lover could know. You're missed.

Finally to our readers, you fill our hearts with joy. Thank you for stopping us to share that you've binged the whole series and we need to write faster. Thank you for sharing with us how Mel and Caro helped you through a difficult time. Thank you for sharing all the parts that made you laugh out loud. Thank you for all the messages, emails, and posts telling us how much you love Caro and Mel. We love to hear from you! If you haven't already done so, please visit our website and sign up to get updates. www.SparkleAbbey.com

If you or someone you know would like to learn more about service dogs, check out www.assistancedogsinternational.org.

Mary Lee and Anita, aka Sparkle Abbey

ABOUT THE AUTHORS

Sparkle Abbey is the pseudonym of two mystery authors (Mary Lee Woods and Anita Carter). They are friends and neighbors as well as co-writers of the *Pampered Pets Mystery Series.* The pen name was created by combining the names of their rescue pets — Sparkle (Mary Lee's cat) and Abbey (Anita's dog). They reside in central Iowa, but if they could write anywhere, you would find them on the beach with their laptops and, depending on the time of day, with either an iced tea or a margarita.

Mary Lee Salsbury Woods is the **"Sparkle"** half of Sparkle Abbey. She is past-president of Sisters in Crime-Iowa and a member of Mystery Writers of America, Romance Writers of America, Kiss of Death, the RWA Mystery Suspense Chapter, Sisters in Crime National, and the SinC Internet group Guppies.

Prior to publishing the *Pampered Pets Mystery Series* with Bell Bridge Books, Mary Lee won first place in the Daphne du Maurier contest, sponsored by the Kiss of Death chapter of RWA, and was a finalist in Murder in the Grove's mystery contest, as well as Killer Nashville's Claymore Dagger contest.

Mary Lee is an avid reader and supporter of public libraries. She lives in Central Iowa with her husband, Tim, and Sparkle, the rescue cat namesake of Sparkle Abbey. In her day job, she is the non-techie in the IT Department. Any spare time she spends reading and enjoying her sons, daughters-in-law, and six grandchildren.

Anita Carter is the **"Abbey"** half of Sparkle Abbey. She is a member of Mystery Writers of America, Romance Writers of America, Kiss of Death, the RWA Mystery Suspense chapter, and Sisters in Crime.

She grew up reading Trixie Belden, Nancy Drew, and the Margo Mystery series by Jerry B. Jenkins (years before his popular *Left Behind* series). Her family is grateful all the years of "fending for yourself" dinners of spaghetti and frozen pizza have finally paid off, even though they haven't exactly stopped.

In Anita's day job, she works for a fitness company. She also lives in Central Iowa with her husband and four children, son-in-law, grandchild, and a rescue dog, Sophie.